DOLLHOUSE

by Kourtney, Kim, and Khloé Kardashian

FICTION
Dollhouse

NONFICTION
Kardashian Konfidential

DOLLHOUSE

KOURTNEY, KIM, AND KHLOÉ
KARDASHIAN

wm

WILLIAM MORROW
An Imprint of HarperCollinsPublishers

DOLLHOUSE. Copyright © 2011 by 2Die4Kourt, Inc., Kimsaprincess, Inc., and KhloMoney, Inc. All rights reserved. Printed in the United States of America. No part of this book may be used or reproduced in any manner whatsoever without written permission except in the case of brief quotations embodied in critical articles and reviews. For information address HarperCollins Publishers, 10 East 53rd Street, New York, NY 10022.

HarperCollins books may be purchased for educational, business, or sales promotional use. For information please write: Special Markets Department, HarperCollins Publishers, 10 East 53rd Street, New York, NY 10022.

A hardcover edition of this book was published in 2011 by William Morrow, an imprint of HarperCollins Publishers.

FIRST WILLIAM MORROW PAPERBACK EDITION PUBLISHED 2012.

Designed by Jamie Lynn Kerner

Library of Congress Cataloging-in-Publication Data has been applied for.

ISBN 978-0-06-206383-0

12 13 14 15 16 OV/RRD 10 9 8 7 6 5 4 3 2 1

To our fans

DOLLHOUSE

PART I

SISTERS

ONE

KAMILLE

Sitting in a café across the street from her family's restaurant, Kamille Romero sipped her açaí berry smoothie and lifted her face to soak in the sun. It was a deliciously warm day, not too humid for August in L.A. She had spent the afternoon at her favorite spa—not one of those New Age-y spas, but a serious, old-school spa run by a scary-efficient Romanian woman named Bogdana. Kamille's arms, legs, and bikini still stung from the honey-scented wax. But it was a good kind of pain, and besides, beauty was painful, right? Waxing and tweezing, like dieting, detoxing, and working out, all hurt.

And they all cost money. She'd had to try two different credit cards to pay her bill at Bogdana's, since it turned out one of them was maxed out. Kamille was going to have to talk to her mother, Kat, about giving her another raise, or at least an advance on her next paycheck. The last time they'd had this not-fun conversation, Kat had actually suggested that Kamille consider cutting back on the weekly spa visits and a few other "luxuries."

Luxuries, seriously? As far as Kamille was concerned, these were all necessities. Kat herself had taught Kamille and her sisters to take pride in their appearance and maintain a strict grooming ritual, including regular hair removal. Just because they were poor now didn't mean they had to be furry and ugly, did it?

At least Kamille made an effort. She couldn't say the same thing about her big sister, Kass, who was naturally pretty but couldn't be bothered to do much with her appearance. (Kass's idea of glam was carrying a purse instead of throwing all her stuff into her USC backpack.) Or their baby sister Kyle, who cared more about looking shocking than stylish. (Fishnets and skull chokers were *so* yesterday.)

Kamille's cell buzzed. She smiled; maybe it was a text from her boyfriend Finn? She hadn't heard from him all day.

But no, it was a superannoying text from her mother: DOLL, WHERE R U?

Frowning, Kamille typed: MY SHIFT STARTS 430.

Kat replied: NO 4! GET YOUR BUTT IN HERE!

What? Kamille rolled her eyes. Her mom could be such a controlling bitch. Ever since she'd opened the restaurant four years ago, just after their father's death, she'd put the girls to work. Which was not cool. At age twenty, Kamille was meant for something bigger and better than waitressing or busing tables. She just wasn't exactly sure what that "something" might be. But her destiny was out there, waiting for her, as sparkly and spectacular as the Kodak Theatre on Oscar Night . . .

Her phone started ringing. The screen lit up: MOM CALL-ING, along with a picture of Kat in her "Hot Mama" T-shirt.

Kamille hit "ignore call" and flagged down the waitress for another smoothie.

DAVID ALEXANDER ROMERO HAD BEEN A FAMOUS FILM producer. But more important, he had been the most awesome dad in the world.

His sudden death had been terrible enough. Kamille was never going to get over that pain, ever. But a few days after his sailing accident, Kat found out that he had secretly invested the family's savings with his best friend, who was a big-deal investment banker to the rich and famous. And that the best friend, now officially a major asshole, had been arrested for committing fraud and leaving all his clients broke—including the Romeros.

Everything changed after that. Kat had to sell their lavish mansion in Beverly Hills and move them to a way more modest house in Los Feliz. Kamille was sixteen then; Kass was seven-teen; and Kyle was twelve. The designer clothes, the expensive family vacations, the fancy parties . . . all that was in the past. The agents, actors, directors, and other Hollywood A-listers who'd always kowtowed to their father suddenly didn't seem to know who Kat and the girls were.

Kamille learned an important life lesson then: that money was power, and that no money meant no power. It was a lesson that haunted her to this day and seriously made her want to scream and throw things—at walls, at people.

Kat, to her credit, didn't curl up and die. Thank God. She used David's life insurance to buy a defunct restaurant in West Hollywood and turn it into Café Romero. Somehow, miraculously, the restaurant was an immediate success. It didn't bring back the millions they'd lost, too bad, but at least they weren't homeless. Although it would have been way better if Kat weren't using her own children as labor. But, whatever.

The next big change was when Kat married her longtime friend, Beau LeBlanc. Fortunately, Beau—a retired Dodgers pitcher—was a nice guy. Occasionally, he even took Kamille's side against Kat when she was being insane (which happened a lot—Kamille and Kass had a private joke that "PMS" stood for "Psychotic Mom Syndrome"). Beau's kids from his previous marriage, Benjamin (aka Benjy) and Brianna (aka Bree), lived with them most of the time, and weren't *too* annoying.

Besides, Kamille and Kass had their own place now, near the family house, so they could come and go as they pleased. And Kass was a great roommate. Sort of. Most of the time.

WHEN KAMILLE STROLLED INTO CAFÉ ROMERO AT 4:35, Kat was going over the evening's menu with her head chef, Fernando. The late-afternoon sun lit up the distressed-yellow walls that always reminded Kamille of their family vacation to Italy, freshman year of high school. The vases of gerbera daisies looked pretty on the mismatched vintage tables that her mother had rescued from some estate sale in OC.

Kamille glanced at her phone. Nothing. She had texted

Finn six times today, and he was still MIA. *Where is he?* she wondered irritably. She wished he was on Twitter so she could spy on him, like she had done with her previous boyfriends (and continued to do sometimes, when she was bored).

"I think we should go with a risotto special," Kat was saying to Fernando. "Let's do something with the new morel mushrooms we just got. How about with some asparagus?"

"A morel-and-asparagus risotto, sounds delish," Fernando agreed. "Let me just check in the kitchen and make sure we have enough stock. I need to get in there and start prepping, anyway."

"Ask Kass about the stock, she's back there doing inventory. I think she made a huge batch last night with the leftover roast chicken?"

"My goodness, is there anything that girl can't do? Hello, angel!" Fernando waved to Kamille. "My, don't you look to die for in that adorable dress? Versace?"

"No, Dolce and Gabbana," Kamille replied. "I got it at Barnee's." She didn't explain that it was from Barnee's (with an *e*) Consignment Shop on Melrose—not the high-end department store Barneys (with a *y*). Of course, she'd had to have it dry-cleaned three times before she wore it, to get rid of the previous owner's lingering BO and cheap, nasty perfume. But she couldn't afford to be picky. "Hey, is there fresh coffee?" she called out to Kat.

"Do you see a Starbucks sign out front? You're thirty-five—no, thirty-six minutes late. Can you type up this menu for me, usual format? Then print out a hundred copies?" Her mother waved a piece of paper at her.

"Kyle's better on the computer," Kamille grumbled.

"Kyle's not here yet. She's even later than you are. Why is it that Kassidy is the only one I can depend on around here?" Kat snapped.

Kamille knotted her fists, stifling several choice swearwords. She was sick-to-death-tired of constantly hearing what a saint Kass was. It had been going on for years, and seriously, who cared? So Kass had been valedictorian in high school. So she was at the top of her class at USC. So she worked long hours at the restaurant, doing everything from waiting tables to organizing the bills to whipping up gourmet fucking chicken stock like some Rachael Ray clone.

Kass was a saint because she had no life. She didn't date; she claimed she was "too busy." She hardly ever drank, which meant that she was superboring during girls' nights out. All she ever did was work and study, study and work. If Kamille did that 24/7, she could be a perfect, overachieving geek, too.

Oh, well. At least there was Kyle, who was even higher on the MSL (aka "Mom's Shit List") than Kamille. Usually.

The kitchen door swung open, and Kass wandered out, poring intently over a legal pad.

"Kass, my daffodil, how much chicken stock do we have?" Fernando called out as he passed her on his way into the kitchen.

"For soup?"

"For risotto. Entrée-size portions."

"More than enough. Mom, we're way low on the gluten-free pasta. I thought you placed an order last week?"

Kat squeezed her eyes shut and began massaging her temples. "Kass, I *really* can't deal with the gluten-free pasta crisis right now. I have *the* biggest headache. And we're out of the house red. And I need to figure out where in the hell your sister Kyle is. Why am I always having to chase you girls down?" She picked up her phone.

"Let's just substitute the McManis Merlot, we have like ten cases," Kass suggested. She came over and gave Kamille a quick hug. "I am so glad to see you," she whispered. "Not to name names, but *someone's* in total, raging PMS mode. And I'm not talking about Fernando."

Giggling, Kamille hugged Kass back. Her sister could always cheer her up, even if she was one of the reasons Kamille needed cheering up to begin with. "Yeah, I kinda figured. How are you? How was your day? I heard you leave the house at like five A.M. or something."

"It wasn't *that* early. But yeah, I wanted to get to the library early to do some reading for my econ class."

"Um, the semester hasn't even started yet?"

"Yeah, I know. I just wanted to get a jump on it."

"Ooo-kay." Kamille knew better than to question her sister's crazy study habits. "Hey, what are you doing later? I'm meeting up with Finn"—she snuck a peek at her phone; still no text; *fuck* him—"and Simone and this new guy Simone's dating, Lars. We're going to this new club."

"I don't know. Maybe." Kass picked up a wineglass from a nearby table and held it up to the light. "You know, I wouldn't call what Simone does 'dating.' That girl is such a slore—honestly, she's like one giant yeast infection."

Kamille raised her eyebrows (which were perfectly shaped versus out-of-control fuzzy, like Kass's). "God, you are such a *bitch*! Besides, you're one to talk. At least she has fun."

"What is *that* supposed to mean? I have fun!"

"Right, uh-huh. When was the last time you—"

"*Girls!*" Kat interrupted, her phone still glued to her ear. "Stop fighting and get back to work! We have a lot to do. Kamille, please get on those menus, now! And, Kass, can you help Fernando with the prep? Goddamn it, Kyle, why are you not picking up? Do I have to implant you with a tracking device, already?"

"P-M-S," Kass whispered to Kamille. They cracked up.

"What's so funny?" Kat snapped.

"Nothing, Mommy!" Kamille trilled.

"Oh, there's my friend Pippa on my call waiting. Did I tell you girls that I invited her and her son, Parker, to our next Sunday Night Dinner? Remember Parker, Kass?"

"Oooh, setup! Love connection! Can I be the maid of honor at your wedding?" Kamille crowed, slapping Kass on the butt.

"Kam, *stop that!*" Kass yelled.

"It is *not* a setup, I thought it would be nice for Kass and Parker to catch up," Kat said defensively. "Kyle Elizabeth Romero, this is the last message I'm going to leave you today!" she shouted into the phone. "Haul your ass into the restaurant right this second, or I am grounding you. *Forever!* Oh, sorry, Pippa, sweetie, I thought that was Kyle's voice mail. What? What do you mean, you need to get an emergency vaginaplasty?"

"A vagina what? Ew, never mind," Kass whispered to Kamille. "And what does she mean, it would be nice for me and Parker to catch up? Is she serious?"

"See, Mom thinks you need a life, too," Kamille teased her.

"If Parker Ashton-Gould is her idea of a 'life,' I'd rather go out with you and the giant yeast infection," Kass retorted. "Just kidding, ha-ha. You know I love you, right? Even though your taste in friends is highly questionable?"

Kamille fake-smiled at Kass. Sometimes she wondered if her sister really *did* love her. Kass could be so mean, so judgmental, so downright *bitchy*.

But maybe that was just how sisters expressed affection?

TWO

KASS

KASS SET HER KEYS ON THE FRONT HALL TABLE, SLID off her shoes, and placed them neatly on the shoe rack in the closet. The house was blissfully silent, i.e., no loud music or loud laughter or loud sex, which meant that Kamille wasn't home yet. Good. She would take advantage of the peace and quiet to get some much-needed R & R. It had been a long night at the restaurant, and she couldn't wait to kick back with a mug of hot apple cider and a biography of Abraham Lincoln she'd been dying to read.

Thank God she'd said no to an evening out with Kamille and her little entourage. It would have been different if it had been just Kamille and her, hanging out at home with some Ben & Jerry's and an old black-and-white movie. But the idea of clubbing with Kamille and Finn and Simone and Simone's latest accessory . . . well, frankly, Abe Lincoln was way better company.

First of all, Kass really didn't understand the appeal of clubs. Who wanted to stand in line for an hour at the mercy of some rude doorman, just to pay a fortune for a watery drink, shout to be heard above bad pop music, and get hit on by losers? (Not that Kass got hit on much—or ever—but still.)

For another thing, Kass *loathed* Simone. She'd always felt this way about her, ever since Kamille and Simone (inexplicably) became friends in sixth grade. Kass knew Simone was trouble the first time they'd all had a sleepover at the Romero house. Kass was thirteen then, and Simone and Kamille were twelve, and there were several other kids at that particular Taco Bell and horror-movie marathon, including boys. Kass got her period for the first time that night (speaking of horror), and she spent hours in the bathroom trying to figure out how to insert a tampon. (This angle or that angle? Was it *supposed* to feel like a torture device?) She'd finally resorted to pads, which were so huge and bulky, like diapers, but at least they didn't hurt.

Unfortunately, the next morning, their old dog, Valentino (God rest his soul), managed to fish several discarded napkins out of the bathroom wastebasket, gnaw them to shreds, and leave the bloody remains scattered all over the house. The she-witch Simone gleefully pointed them out to the sleepover guests; she also identified them as Kass's, chanting stupid songs about crimson waves and cotton ponies. Kamille had actually laughed along with everyone else—for a second, anyway, before yelling at Simone to shut the fuck up and helping Kass to clean up the mess.

Simone had always brought out the worst in Kamille.

And as for Finn . . . Kass had made it a point not to get too close to any of Kamille's boyfriends because she went through so many of them, so quickly. Pretty much one every three months, like a new diet trend or a new workout routine. Each time, it was the same, with Kamille announcing ecstatically that [fill in the blank] was absolutely and undeniably The One. Then some major drama would happen, and there would be a tearful, devastating breakup . . . after which the pattern would repeat itself.

Kamille never had a problem getting a boyfriend. With her deep blue eyes, voluptuous body, and wild, curly auburn mane, she was drop-dead gorgeous. (When the Romero girls were growing up, people would call her the "pretty" sister, then hastily add that Kass was the "smart" one, as though that was supposed to make up for the implied insult.) Kamille's problem was getting (and keeping) a boyfriend who really and truly cared about her. Why did she always seem to attract jerks with commitment issues?

Kass sighed. Relationships really were more trouble than they were worth. It was a good thing that she herself had chosen to focus on her education. Straight A's were forever. Men most definitely were not.

Her cell buzzed. It was a text from Kamille.

SO FUN HERE CUTE GUYS COME MEET US!

"Right, uh-huh," Kass muttered. Heading down the hall, she lied-slash-typed: SORRY IN BED ALREADY. LOVE U!

No response. Whatever. Kass tucked the phone into her jeans pocket and proceeded through the living room, randomly picking up empty coffee cups (Kamille's) and Baja Fresh bags (Kamille's) and a pair of red stilettos (Kamille's). The decor of the house exactly represented the total split in the two sisters' personalities, i.e., part flea-market vintage (Kass) and part Z Gallerie (Kamille). Kass hated wasting money; why spend two hundred dollars on a new chair when the same item could be had for five dollars at a garage sale, slightly used? Conversely, Kamille hated "other people's old stuff," claiming that they always came with mystery stains and nasty smells.

In this way, the two of them had been arguing and compromising and sharing the cute little Spanish-style bungalow for the last year. Okay, so Kamille wasn't always easy. And she really did need to stop putting all her energy into men and start focusing on what she wanted to do with the rest of her life. But she was Kass's sister and best friend. They shared everything: their secrets, their hopes, their dreams, and their frustrations, especially about the other members of their family. Kass absolutely couldn't imagine *not* living with her—dirty coffee cups and skanky friends and all.

KASS WOKE UP TO THE SOUND OF VERY, VERY LOUD SEX.

"Oh my God, *yes!*" a female voice cried out. "Oh, yeah, faster. *Faster!*"

Kass sat up and peered groggily at the alarm clock: 3:32 A.M. The sound was coming from the living room. Kamille and Finn must be at it on the couch. Really, was this necessary?

But the voice didn't sound like Kamille's.

Then Kass heard another sound through the *other* wall—the wall that separated her bedroom from Kamille's. It was the steady, rhythmic squeaking of a mattress. More sex. Wait—did that mean *two* hookups were going on simultaneously?

"Oh . . . my . . . God!"
"Oh, yeah, that's it!"
"Mmmmmm . . ."
"Harder . . ."

Kass squeezed her eyes shut and covered her ears with her hands, trying to block out the stereophonic X-rated noises. She tried, too, not to think about that other time, back when she was sixteen and Kamille and Simone were fifteen. Kamille and Simone had dragged Kass to some house party way across town in Hidden Hills, and it hadn't ended well, with Kamille and Simone drunk out of their minds and the girl who had given them a ride to the party, Willow, completely passed out. Kamille had somehow convinced Kass to drive them all home in Willow's parents' Mercedes minivan, even though Kass only had her learner's permit and had never driven on a highway. Kass could still recall how terrified she felt, driving down the 405, convinced that she was going to get pulled over any second—or that she was going to crash the superexpensive car—while Kamille made out with some boy in the backseat, and Simone did more than make out with a second boy (Kass could see her grinding away on his lap in her rearview mirror), and Willow slept way in the back in the Burberry dog bed, her snoring mingling with the two couples' moaning and groaning . . .

"Shit," Kass whispered to herself.

Why did everyone else always get to have all the fun?

THREE

KYLE

"COULD YOU PLEASE PASS THE BEEF STEW"—KAT paused—"Wyatt, is it?"

"It's *White*. White Castle," replied Kyle's most excellent date for tonight's Sunday Nightmare Dinner, which is what she called these weekly torture sessions. Tonight it was the whole family—Kyle and her sisters, Kass and Kamille; their two stepsibs, Benjy and Bree; the parents, Kat and Beau (who was technically not a parent but a stepparent)—plus Kat's obnoxious friend Pippa Ashton-Gould and Pippa's extremely lame son, Parker.

And, of course, White. As he lifted the heavy tureen, Kyle noticed her mother's gaze falling on his bare, vampire-pale arm, covered as it was with an assortment of not-very-PG tat-

toos and what might or might not be several track marks. The
min pins, Coco and Chanel, bounded up to the table and went
into high-octane begging mode.

"White Castle! That's a supercool name! Does that mean
you love hamburgers, then?" Bree said, stuffing a buttered roll
into her mouth. At ten, she was insanely chirpy and friendly.
She wasn't too unbearable, for a little stepsister.

"Actually, I'm a vegan. See?" White pointed to his T-shirt,
which had a picture of a headless, bloody chicken and the
words DEAD MEAT on it. "That's our band. I sing lead. Hey,
we're playing at the Bad Touch Lounge over on Sunset this
Wednesday. Midnight show. Y'all should check it out."

"Can I go? Can I go?" Bree squealed.

"*No!*" Kat and Beau said at the same time. "School night,"
Beau added feebly.

"I find vegans so fascinating!" Pippa Ashton-Gould piped
up, leaning toward White and giving him a bird's-eye view of
her rock-hard boob job. Pippa had always reminded Kyle of a
dead monkey, with her surgically thin, spray-tanned body. She
had a way of coming on to younger guys as though she actually had a chance, which she didn't. It was so pathetic, how
old people like Pippa and Kat tried to hang on to the dinosaur
remains of their sexuality. They were like fossils.

"Well, frankly, if you don't believe in eating animals, veg-
anism is the only tenable position," Pippa's son, Parker, added.
"Conventional vegetarianism is a morally murky middle
ground. Animals still have to die in order for milk and eggs to
get produced. So I say, either be a vegan or do like I do and be
unrepentantly carnivorous! Eat meat!" He speared a piece of
beef and chomped down on it gleefully.

What a fucking moron, Kyle thought irritably.

Bree stared in horror at her glass of milk. "There's dead animals in here?" she cried out.

"No, honey, there's no dead animals in there! Drink up!" Forcing a smile, Kat turned to Kyle. "Sweetheart, you didn't tell me your friend was a vegan. I would have made something else," she said through clenched teeth.

"I'm okay, Mrs., uh, Camero," White reassured her. "I'm kinda hungover, so I'm not superhungry, anyway."

Kat shot Kyle a scathing look that was all "Are you serious, bringing *that* home?" Kyle knew that look well. She aimed to please every Sunday night, inviting over whatever hookup, friend, or total stranger, male or female, was bound to shock her mother the most. (Guests were part of the Sunday Nightmare Dinner tradition.) Last week, it had been the sixteen-year-old daughter of a hotel magnate, who had a reputation for hooking up with older, married men. (Kat had seated her *far* away from Beau.) The week before, it had been a homeless teenager Kyle found in Griffith Park. Unfortunately, Kat had screwed things up by actually feeling sorry for the girl, giving her clean clothes and money and finding a social worker to help her. Oh, well.

Of course, Kyle got the scathing look on other days of the week as well. She liked to think of it as a game: new and exciting ways to Piss Off Mom. Who deserved it. Sometimes the game got old, but mostly it was entertaining. It was definitely better than trying to get along with her, like Kyle's ass-kissing sisters.

Speaking of . . .

"Mommy and Beau, did I tell you? My friend Simone said

there's a job opening at her PR firm!" Kamille bubbled. "It's part-time, and it doesn't pay very much. But she gets to go to the coolest parties, and she meets all these celebrities, too! I was thinking I might apply."

"I thought you were going to take singing lessons so you could be the next *American Idol*," Kyle reminded her. "Oh, no, that was *two* Sundays ago. Last Sunday, you were going to move to New York City and intern for some nobody fashion designer you friended on Facebook."

"Okay, Kyle, you know what? Fuck. You," Kamille snapped.

Kat glared. "Kamille, please! Language! And, Kyle, could you be a little more supportive of your sister?"

"Yeah. Just because I don't have my whole life planned out like Miss OCD," Kamille said, casting a sideways glance at Kass.

Kass frowned. "Uh, thanks?"

Kat turned to Parker. "What Kamille means is, Kass is doing so well at USC! She's about to start her junior year there, and she's double-majoring in business plus film and television!" She turned to Kass. "And, sweetie, did you know that Parker graduated from Harvard in June? With a degree in geology?"

Gag! Their mother was so obvious about fixing up Parker with Kass, it was painful. On the other hand, Kass *did* need to get laid, so points to Mom for trying, even though on a scale of one to ten, the chemistry between Kass and Parker was about negative two.

"Yeah, I remember you were into rocks in kindergarten, too," Kass said to Parker without looking at him. "I think you threw one at my new tricycle and dented the handlebar."

"Oh, right, that was funny!" Kamille giggled.

Kass whirled around and punched Kamille in the arm. "It was *not* funny, I loved that tricycle!"

"Hey, that *hurts*!"

"Not as much as this!" Kass leaned over and yanked on Kamille's hair. Kamille did the same to Kass. What were they, three years old? They started laughing, although there was an edge to their laughter.

"Who wants some dessert?" Kat said brightly. "It's lemon cake! We always have it, because it was David's—the girls' father's—favorite," she explained to White.

"Cool. Is it vegan?" he asked.

"Actually, it has a couple of eggs in it," Kat replied.

"Eggs, yeah . . . my friend calls them 'chicken periods,'" White remarked.

Kat gasped. Beau put his hand on her arm, probably to keep her from totally losing her shit. *Awesome.* Kyle reminded herself to bring White to these dinners more often.

"We've got some sorbet in the freezer. I'll bring that out for our guest White here," Beau said hastily. "Benjy, honey, you want to help me clear?"

"Sure, Dad." Benjy, who had not said a word during the entire dinner, pushed back his chair and stood up. Kyle scrutinized him. He had been her stepbrother for almost four years now, and he still remained a mystery to her. Sure, she hadn't exactly bothered to be friendly to him. But why should she? They had nothing in common, other than the fact that they were both juniors at Wesley Eastman Academy. He was a straight-A student and in general a big, fat nerd who was always reading books or rehearsing lines for his dumb drama club. He and Bree lived with them except when they were in Brentwood with their mom. Unless the mom happened to be away at an ashram or in rehab, which was kind of often.

"I never touch dessert because I have to watch my girlish figure," Pippa said, winking at White.

Okay, enough of the Cougar Show. "Come on, I didn't give you a tour of the house yet," Kyle said, grabbing White's hand.

"A what?"

"Come on!"

"Be back here in five minutes for cake," Kat ordered Kyle.

"Can I go with you, Ky?" Bree begged.

"No, Brie Cheese. You stay here, I'll be right back."

Or not. Once in the hallway, Kyle tried to think of where she could take White that would have the most impact when Kat came looking for them. They could skinny-dip in the pool. Or they could go upstairs and make out on the parents' bed. Despite his freakish tattoos and raccoon-colored hair, White wouldn't be *too* repulsive to touch. Would he?

"Hey, what's this?" White was staring at an ancient photo of Beau on the wall.

"What? Oh, that's just Beau," Kyle said dismissively. She glanced down the hall. Her mother had recently bought an Oriental rug for her home office. Maybe *that* would be a better place to get down and dirty with White?

Kyle turned to him, smiling provocatively and touching his chest. But he seemed to have lost interest in her all of a sudden. "Dude, your dad's Beau *LeBlanc*?" he burst out. "This picture's from the World Series, right? From like twenty years ago?"

"Beau is *not* my dad," Kyle said irritably. She tugged on White's arm. "Hey, you wanna—"

"Do you think he'd sign my shirt?" White said, hurrying back to the dining room. "Fuck, man! What's it like having a famous baseball player for a dad?"

"He is *not* my dad!" Kyle repeated. But White was already gone.

Crap!

FOUR

KAMILLE

'M TELLING YOU, HE'S A JERK. YOU NEED TO BREAK UP!"
Simone declared.

"What?" Kamille glanced up from her phone and regarded her friend. Simone seemed to be really, really worked up about something. Of course, this wasn't unusual. Simone was a raging drama queen, which was one of the reasons Kamille liked having her around, because it made her feel calm and sane in comparison.

"Carlos and I were at Voyeur last night, and—"

"Carlos? What happened to Lars?"

"Lars? Ohmigod, we broke up like a week ago. He's ancient history. Anyway, I saw Finn at Voyeur, but he totally didn't see me. He was making out with another girl. They were practically dry-humping in their booth!"

"I don't think so. Finn told me he was working last night."

"Well, he lied. Besides, didn't you see the picture I texted you?"

"What picture?"

Simone shook her head and grabbed Kamille's phone from her. As she scrolled, Kamille peered around the Coffee Bean & Tea Leaf, which was uncharacteristically empty for a Friday morning. It was just Kamille and Simone, half a dozen tourists, a lone nun, and a couple who was way overdoing it with the PDA. Really, in front of a nun?

There was also a guy in the corner who had been checking out Kamille for the last half hour. Of course, she got checked out by all sorts of guys all the time. Still, this one was older than usual—forties?—and way better dressed, in a dreamy gray Armani suit she had seen on that hot Spanish model in *Vogue*.

The guy had arrived in a silver Rolls, chauffeured. It was still parked out front, presumably waiting for him to finish his latte. Was he a rich businessman? Kamille had to admit she was a little curious, even though he absolutely wasn't her type.

Besides, she already had a boyfriend. Didn't she?

"Here!" Simone thrust Kamille's phone back at her. "This is your proof right here."

Kamille stared at the screen. The picture was kind of grainy and out of focus. But upon closer inspection, it *did* look like Finn kissing some skanky redhead who was wearing a—wait, was she wearing anything? Were those her boobs?

"The beeyotch flashed him, and that's when he decided that he couldn't resist her charms anymore," Simone explained, as though reading Kamille's mind. "Okay, so, can we please dump his pathetic ass and move on already? I could *tell* he was a cheater the first time I met him. I have a sixth sense about these things."

Kamille felt heat rush to her cheeks. "There's got to be some explanation."

"Yeah, sweetie, there's an explanation. The explanation is, your soon-to-be-ex-boyfriend is a sorry piece of shit who can't keep it in his pants."

"No, I mean . . . look, maybe he was drunk. Or maybe she threw herself at him and he was trying to push her away."

Simone rolled her eyes. "Girlfriend. Honestly? We need to organize a man intervention for you. You're cutting him way too much slack."

"You don't know Finn as well as I do. He's not like that. Besides, I'm seeing him tonight. I'll ask him what happened, and I'm sure he'll tell me everything."

"You are *way* too trusting," Simone said irritably. She peered at her watch. "Listen, I gotta bail. Seriously, though . . . is the sex *that* good? Because I don't know why you bother with an a-hole like him when you could have any guy on the planet." She rose to her feet.

Kamille blushed and turned away. The truth was, the sex *wasn't* that good. Although maybe it was her fault, not Finn's? He was the twelfth guy she'd gone to bed with, and she hadn't been able to enjoy herself with any of them. Was there something wrong with her? Did she need to see a shrink? Or was she a lesbian deep down and just didn't know it? There *was* that time she and her friend Marlena drank too many margaritas at that house party in Bel Air and made out, which was kind of fun. But . . . for the most part, she liked guys. She just didn't like having sex with any of the ones she'd been with.

Of course, her first experience—with Jeremy Weinstein, freshman year—hadn't been an auspicious start. They'd done it at his house while his parents were in Aspen, and when she went to the bathroom afterward, to pee, she realized in horror that his condom was stuck inside of her. *Deep* inside. She extracted it with a pair of tweezers from her makeup bag, flushed it down the toilet, and washed her hands with an entire bottle of antibacterial soap plus the hottest water she could bear. Back in the living room, Jeremy was freaking out because he couldn't find the condom anywhere, and she was too mortified to tell him what had happened to it. Yeah, romantic.

Simone checked her watch again. "Okay, I'm now officially fifteen minutes late for work," she said. "Oh, hey, are you still interested in that part-time receptionist thing? Because you need to send me your résumé, like, yesterday. I think my boss's niece might be applying."

"Yeah, maybe. I don't know. I think I might pass." The more Kamille thought about it, the less exciting the job sounded, answering phones and greeting clients. Even if some of the clients *were* celebrities. For one thing, it meant that she would actually have to wake up early and go into an office. It was bad enough, having to show up at Café Romero for her shifts and answering to her mother the tyrant. But having a *real* boss who could legit-order her around? And fire her if she didn't comply?

Besides, professionally speaking, Kamille wanted more glamour and less manual labor. And she wanted to make a ton of money, too, so she could stop being poor and go back to the lifestyle she used to have, when her father was alive. Surely, there had to be something out there that met those simple requirements?

"Okay, well, let me know if you change your mind," Simone said. "Hey, you wanna do something this weekend? How about Hyde?"

Kamille hesitated. The last time she'd been at Hyde with Simone, her friend had gotten so wasted that she'd done something truly unimaginable. At one point late in the evening, Simone asked Kamille to hand her a bottle of gin that was on the table. Kamille did, at the same time noticing that Simone seemed to be sitting in a weird position, sort of half slipping off the booth. To Kamille's shock, Simone then proceeded to tip the gin bottle upside-down between her legs, letting the liquor gush out. It turned out that she was in the process of peeing on the floor—she wasn't wearing panties, and her minidress was hiked up around her hips—and was covering up the smell with the gin so no one would notice. She explained that she hadn't wanted to bother with the crazy-long ladies' room line.

"Maybe the Roxbury would be better," Kamille said delicately.

"Whatever. Text me, okay? And don't forget. Break. Up. With. Him." Simone blew a kiss and took off.

Kamille made a face and turned her attention back to the picture of Finn and the red-haired skank. Was Simone right? Was she too trusting when it came to men? Jeremy Weinstein was secretly hooking up with Sarah what's-her-name for three months before Kamille found out, even though everyone tried

"Right, then. I look forward to hearing from you, Kamille Romero."

Kamille waited until Giles had gotten into his silver Rolls-Royce and disappeared down the street. Then she picked up her phone and Googled "Sinclair Modeling Management."

There was his photo. Okay, so maybe he *wasn't* a serial killer.

Then she saw his client list, and her jaw dropped. The list included Svetlana Sergeyev, who was Kamille's number one favorite supermodel, ever . . . plus the hot Spanish model who had worn Giles's Armani suit in *Vogue* . . . plus a dozen other names she recognized.

"Holy . . . fucking . . . shit," she said out loud.

The nun glanced up from her Bible and Earl Grey tea and stared sharply at her.

Kamille stifled a giggle. She didn't care. She was going to become a famous supermodel!

FIVE

KASS

KASS SLIPPED ON HER RAY-BANS AS SHE WALKED OUT of the Marshall School of Business and reread her econ notes. The professor had sprung a pop quiz on them, on antitrust laws, and she was worried that she might have gotten one of the answers wrong. She knew she had an almost perfect average in that class, from the previous two quizzes. But still. Almost perfect was not the same as perfect, and besides, the fall semester had just begun. A lot could go wrong between now and December.

The palm-tree-lined walk outside the building was swarming with students rushing off to their next class. It was a hot, sultry day, typical for late August in SoCal. On the lawn, a group of girls was sunbathing in bikinis and bobbing their heads, connected by a complex network of white earbuds. She recognized a few faces from her class. She couldn't imagine cutting, especially with a teacher like Professor Mueller, who took no prisoners when it came to attendance. Kass herself had not missed a single class in her three years at USC, except once when she had a temperature of 103. And even then, her mother had to force her to stay home, because James Cameron was guest-lecturing in her film class that day.

Kamille had been right when she made that (bitchy) comment several Sunday Night Dinners ago. Kass *did* have her whole life planned out, or at least the career part of it, and it involved both stellar attendance and stellar grades. She was going to graduate summa cum laude—with highest honors— with a double major in business administration and film and television production.

Eventually, she would use her degree to follow in her father's footsteps and become a producer. In the meantime, her USC education was helping her with her job at the restaurant, which was badly in need of careful management. Her mother's forte was creating menus, not spreadsheets.

Her cell buzzed. It was a call from Kamille.

"KASSIE!" Kass had to hold her phone away from her ear because her sister was screaming. *"GUESS WHAAAAAT?"*

"I can hear you, doll. What's going on? Are you all right?"

"I'm better than all right. Guess who I just met?"

"Taylor Lautner?"

"Better! Giles Sinclair!"

"I'm sorry—who?"

"He's a modeling agent, and he represents Svetlana Sergeyev, can you believe it? He came up to me at a Coffee Bean

& Tea Leaf, it was so random, and he wanted to talk to me about modeling. I was, like, 'Get lost' at first, but then I realized he was legit. And guess what, Kass? He wants me to do a test shoot! You know what that is, right? It's a professional photo shoot so he can get sample pictures of me to send to, like, advertising agencies. Advertising agencies that work for fashion designers and makeup companies and stuff. I'm gonna be a model!"

Kass's head was spinning. "Wait. *Who* is this guy? And I know what a test shoot is."

"I just told you. He's a modeling agent. He's one of the biggest in the business."

"How do you spell his name? Let me check him out."

"I already did. He's got the coolest website ever."

"Spell it for me, anyway."

Kass could hear the heavy sigh on the other end of the line as Kamille spelled the name. Hmm. Giles Sinclair. It sounded faux British and pretentious.

"I've gotta get new clothes for the test shoot, and get my hair and makeup done, too," Kamille was prattling on. "Do you think Mom'll lend me the money? Or I could just put it on my credit cards. I think? Models get paid a ton, right? I should be able to pay off the balance in like a month or two, tops. Or maybe I should—"

"*Kam!*" Kass pressed her fingers against her temple. "Sweetie, slow down. Look, I have to run to the library. Can we talk later? What are you doing tonight?"

There was a long silence. "*Wellll* . . . I was supposed to have dinner with Finn. But he just texted me and said he had to reschedule 'cause something came up, blah, blah, blah." Kamille didn't sound happy.

Kass sensed that there was more to this story than what Kamille was telling her. She'd have to get the scoop later. "Okay, well, great! So you're free? You wanna meet back at the house? We can order in pizza and talk about what this Giles person is proposing, and make a pros and cons list for you."

"A pros and cons list? What for?"

"Just trust me. You need to think these things through carefully. I'll see you tonight, okay?"

"Um, okay."

"Love you, doll!"

"Love you, too, doll!"

Hanging up, Kass Googled "Giles Sinclair" and went through his website, twice. Okay, so he was for real.

She continued down the walk, suddenly in a foul mood. But why? She should be happy for Kamille, who had been *discovered*, for God's sake. It was like something out of Hollywood legend, like actress Lana Turner being discovered at the Top Hat Café while skipping class and drinking a Coke. (So maybe skipping class *did* pay off sometimes?)

The problem was, amazing stuff *always* happened to Kamille, and she never had to lift a finger. Like in high school, when the drama teacher gave her a lead in *Peter Pan,* and she didn't even have to audition. Kass, on the other hand, had to work like a dog—not just going to college but putting in long hours at the restaurant—and so far, she hadn't hit the jackpot.

Of course, her efforts would surely pay off someday, and she would be wildly successful. And rich. She didn't particularly care about the "rich" part, except that she had another, top-secret dream that she had never shared with anyone, not even Kamille, with whom she shared pretty much everything.

Her top-secret dream was to buy back their old house in Beverly Hills, if and when it went on the market again. Her father had bought it for the family when Kass was a baby. Her mother had to sell it after he died because she needed the money, plus she couldn't afford the maintenance.

But someday, Kass was going to honor her father's memory by taking it back. Plus, she missed that house desperately. Not because it was a big, fancy mansion—she was a practical person and not particularly interested in luxuries. But that house on Mulholland Drive was the Romero home. It was meant to be in the Romero family, now and forever.

Kass felt someone tapping her shoulder. She turned and saw a familiar-looking guy. A familiar-looking, very *cute* guy.

"Um, hey," the guy said, smiling shyly. "You dropped this."

"Dropped what?"

The guy held out her econ notebook.

Kass was momentarily rattled. She never lost track of anything, ever. How did she manage to drop her incredibly important econ notes?

"Thanks," she said, flustered. "Where did you—"

"Oh, just outside Marshall. You were on the phone. Quiz was a bitch, wasn't it?"

"What quiz?"

The guy looked amused. "Econ. I sit a couple of rows over from you. Professor Mueller was wearing his Elvis Costello glasses today."

Kass laughed. "Yeah, I think he thinks they make him look really cool. Or something."

The guy held out his hand. "I'm Eduardo, by the way."

"Kassidy. Everyone calls me Kass."

"Nice to meet you, Kass. Hey, you wanna grab a coffee? We could go over those Supreme Court decisions he mentioned. I'm sensing another pop quiz on Monday."

Kass regarded Eduardo. He seemed nice. And smart. And definitely cute. But she really did have to get to the library to . . . what was she doing there, again? Oh, yeah, checking out some books on globalization. Which could wait. But her day was so jam-packed already. If she postponed the library errand, when would she be able to squeeze it in? She had her Spanish class in an hour, then her small-business management study group, then a private screening of a new Kathryn Bigelow movie at the film school, then a brief stop at the restaurant to go over some paperwork, then her girls' night in with Kamille . . .

Eduardo was staring at her with his really adorable dark brown eyes. *Why the hell not?* Kass thought, and was about to say yes to the coffee when she changed her mind. Again.

"I'd love to, but I have like a million things to do," she said finally.

"No problem. Maybe another time. See you in class on Monday." He smiled and walked away.

As Kass watched him go, she felt a pang of regret. But the feeling was temporary. A second later, she was already thinking about those globalization books.

SIX

KAT

"SO I JUST WANTED TO EXPRESS THAT WE HERE AT Wesley Eastman Academy continue to be concerned about Kyle," Mr. Leibowitz said gravely. "We're barely into this academic year, and it already promises to be a repeat of last year."

Kat leaned back in the incredibly stiff, uncomfortable leather chair—it was probably some priceless antique, judging from the rest of the decor in the headmaster's office as well as the exorbitant tuition the school charged—and turned to Beau with a frown. He reached over and squeezed her hand reassuringly. But she could tell that he was just as worried as she was, inside.

And was the room insanely overheated? Or was it her? Kat

picked up a copy of the latest Wesley Eastman newsletter and began fanning herself. She wondered if it might be hot flashes. Great. So she had menopause and aging and all that crap to deal with on top of everything else . . .

"All of her teachers say that she is an exceptionally bright, talented, very creative young woman who simply fails to apply herself," Mr. Leibowitz went on. "If she chose to, she could be a straight-A student here. But in this first week alone, she skipped class twice, she failed to turn in *any* of her homework . . . and she did *this*." He slid a sheet of paper across the desk. "It's a precalculus quiz. Or it was supposed to be, anyway."

Kat leaned forward, and so did Beau. On the piece of paper were a dozen equations that might as well have been in Martian, they were that foreign to Kat. (Math had never been her strong suit in school.) But Kyle hadn't bothered solving any of them. Instead of answers in the blank lines, there were hand-scribbled pictures of two dogs: running, eating, sleeping, playing, and . . .

Kat squinted. And gasped. Oh my *God,* were they having *sex*?

Beau dug around in his pocket for his reading glasses. "Are those dogs, honey? Hey, maybe she was drawing Coco and Chanel." He smiled at Mr. Leibowitz. "We have these two min pins at home. Miniature pinschers. Are you familiar with the breed? Real friendly, and real good with kids. Well, most of the time, as long as they're not—"

"*Beau!*" Kat stabbed her finger at the picture. "I don't *think* that's Coco and Chanel. At least I hope not! I mean, not that there's anything *wrong* with two females having . . . that is . . ." She blushed and willed herself to stop speaking immediately.

"What, darlin'? *Oh!*" Beau peered through his glasses at the humping dogs. "O-*kay*. Whoa! Not sure what to say about that one. Mr. Leibowitz, we apologize for our daughter. Believe me, we'll have a frank talking-to with her as soon as we get home."

"Yes, well. That would be a good idea. Perhaps if you could redirect her focus to her academics in a positive way, she would benefit from her sense of achievement and stop feeling the need to . . . act out, shall we say?"

"You mean, if she started trying harder in her classes and getting good grades, she would feel better about herself and stop being such a royal pain in the . . . you know?" Kat said tactfully.

"Exactly."

After the meeting was over—they thanked Mr. Leibowitz for his time and promised him they would "take decisive measures"—Kat and Beau headed outside and sat down on a bench in the courtyard. The school was picture-postcard pretty, a sprawling ten-acre campus with a view of the Santa Monica Mountains. Kat loved the Spanish Mission–style architecture of the building, with its cream stucco walls, sweeping arches, and clay tile roofs. Off in the distance, the boys' track team was doing laps.

Kat and Beau just held hands for a long moment and didn't speak. "I'm exhausted," she said finally.

"I know, sweetheart. I don't know how you do it all, running the restaurant and taking care of the kids and taking care of me and—"

Kat shook her head. "No, that's not it. Well, yes, of course,

I'm exhausted by all that. But what I really meant was, *Kyle* exhausts me. She exhausts me to the very core. I've tried to be there for her, to reach out to her, but it's like she's hellbent on pissing me off. Pissing *us* off. But mostly me. Like all those crazies she brings to our Sunday Night Dinners. And not taking her job at the restaurant seriously. And why do we bother paying a fortune for her private school tuition—money we don't exactly have—when she's just wasting it all away? Honestly!" She buried her face in her hands.

"Darlin', darlin' . . ." Beau wrapped his arm around her shoulders and hugged her tightly. "It's gonna be okay. She's a teenager. She'll outgrow this. If I recall, you weren't above a little misbehavin' when you were younger." He laughed softly.

Kat sat up and glared at him. Was he talking about the things they used to do when they first met, when she was seventeen? And he was a rookie pitcher for the Dodgers, fresh out of Tulane? How she used to sneak out of her parents' house after they were asleep so she could spend the night with him, and sneak back in before dawn?

Or was he talking about what happened later, after she was married to David?

Whatever it was, she didn't want to talk about it now. "What are we going to do about her?" she said helplessly.

"Let's do what the good headmaster suggested. Let's help her to get her grades up."

"Sure. But how?"

"Why don't we hire a tutor to help her out?" Beau suggested.

"Oh!" Kat lit up. "That's actually a really good idea!"

Beau chuckled. "I guess I'll take that as a compliment?"

"It is! So how do we find a tutor? I guess we could go online, or maybe Pippa knows somebody, or—"

"What about Benjy?"

"Our Benjy?"

"*Our* Benjy. Lookit . . . he's a straight-A student. He and Kyle are in a lot of the same classes here, so he'd be familiar with the material. He's got a load of patience. And he's been talking about wanting to make some extra money, right?"

"True. I was thinking he might want to bus tables at the restaurant. But I guess tutoring would be a better fit for him?"

"Exactly."

Kat nodded slowly. Beau was right. Benjy was the perfect candidate for the job.

Of course, they would have to talk to Kyle about all this ASAP, informing her that she was going to have to commit to these tutoring sessions with Benjy (if he agreed to them), put her nose to the grindstone, and achieve a respectable GPA, or else. Kat was not looking forward to that conversation. Frankly, she didn't look forward to any conversations with Kyle these days.

Kat remembered when Kyle was born, how sweet she was, how she just wanted to nurse and cuddle all day long. Her first word was *mama,* and when she was three, she told Kat in her adorable toddler lisp that she was her "bestest friend, forever and ever and ever." When she was in elementary school, Kat and David used to call her "Cinderella" because she was so helpful and well behaved and eager to please.

When did things go wrong? The darkness seemed to have seeped into Kyle's personality soon after David's death. Kyle had adored her father, who had pampered her maybe more than the older girls because she was the baby. In some ways, Kyle had taken his death the hardest, by not grieving properly or giving herself a chance to heal. She hadn't even cried at the funeral, or any time after, that Kat was aware of.

When Kyle was thirteen, Kat caught her smoking pot in her room. Actually, not just smoking pot . . . she was showing little Bree, age seven, how to roll a joint.

When Kyle was fourteen, she started sneaking out of the house, stuffing pillows under her blankets and slipping out a side door. Once, Kat caught her trying to sneak back in, dressed in a sequined minidress that barely covered her privates and carrying a fake ID with the name Bobby Brown, age twenty-one.

And worst of all . . . when Kyle was fifteen, and Kat and Beau were away for the weekend, she stole the family's brand-new navy Range Rover and drove it to a P. F. Chang's in Marina del Rey to meet up with a bunch of friends. Unfortunately, the restaurant happened to share a parking lot with a hotel, and some woman happened to be in one of the hotel rooms at the time, hooking up with a man who wasn't her husband. The husband showed up and angrily set fire to the boyfriend's car. The Rover was parked next to that car and caught fire as well. Kyle had been so afraid of Kat and Beau's wrath that she hadn't come home for almost forty-eight hours. And rightly so; they ended up grounding her for three months. (Kat had wanted *six* months, except that Beau had pointed out to her—privately, gently—that the incident had occurred on the exact anniversary of David's death.)

And now Kyle was sixteen. And things didn't seem to be getting any better.

But what was the solution? Kat had suggested therapy to Kyle several times, including family therapy, and Kyle had adamantly refused. Maybe a new school? Or music lessons, to give her a creative outlet? What was the answer?

She sniffed and dabbed at her eyes. Beau tipped her face up to his. "Honey? You okay?" he whispered.

"I'm fine."

"No, you're not. You're crying. What is it?"

"It's just that . . . oh, I don't know. This stuff really gets to me. Kyle, the kids."

"Which kids?"

"It's mostly Kyle. But I'm worried about Kamille and Kass, too. Kamille thinks she's going to become a supermodel, which sounds totally pie-in-the-sky to me. I mean, of course she's gorgeous. But that's like me wanting to become a four-star Michelin chef or having my own Food Network show. And Kass—well, Kass is perfect, which is a problem, because really, that girl needs to loosen up and live a little, and I don't know why she and Parker Ashton-Gould didn't hit it off." Kat sighed. "Plus, I think I might be going through menopause."

"Menopause? Um, aren't you a little young for that?"

"I'm forty-four. Pippa's my age, and she's been getting symptoms for a while now. Like just the other day, she was telling me that she's been feeling really, really dry down there, and—"

"Whoa, ixnay! Too much information!"

Kat laughed. "Sorry."

"So does this mean our sex life is going to, you know, slow down?" Beau joked.

"Is *that* all you care about?" Kat punched him in the arm.

"Yes." Beau leaned over and kissed her neck. And her ear.

"Beau LeBlanc, what are you doing?"

As his mouth found hers, she wished they were alone some-where, and not in a very public courtyard at a high school. Their *children's* high school. "Okay, enough," she protested feebly. "Mr. Leibowitz is going to have us arrested."

"Good. Let him," Beau whispered, unbuttoning the top button of her blouse.

"Beau!"

Menopause was definitely not going to slow them down.

SEVEN

KAMILLE

KAMILLE'S PHONE BEGAN RINGING IN THE MIDDLE OF *SOME Like It Hot,* which was one of her (and Kass's) favorite films of all time. She and Simone were hanging out at the house, drinking a pitcher of midori sours and discussing who looked hotter in a dress, Tony Curtis or Jack Lemmon. Kamille had left Kass a message telling her to get her butt home ASAP so she could watch the rest of the movie with them.

"Is that your loser sister calling?" Simone sniped as she tossed back the rest of her drink. She poured herself another, picked up her own phone, and began texting.

"That's nice, Simone. You talk like that about Kassie again, I'll beat the shit out of you." Seeing Giles Sinclair's name on the caller ID, Kamille hit the talk button. "Hello?"

"Kamille? It's Giles Sinclair. Do you have a minute? I have some news."

Kamille sat up. The guy worked fast! She had met him exactly a week ago; since then, he had arranged for her to do a test shoot at a supercool photo studio in Culver City and promised to send the pictures out to prospective clients. And he was already calling her with news?

Kamille dug around for the remote, which was buried under a pile of silk pillows, and turned down the volume. "Hey, Giles. What's up?" she said eagerly.

"Jeunesse is launching a new perfume, and they want to use you for their ad campaign!"

"*Whaaaaaat?*" Kamille jumped to her feet. Jeunesse, the famous French perfume maker, wanted *her* for their new ad? "Are you joking? You're not joking, are you?" she said breathlessly to Giles.

Giles chuckled. "No, love, I'm not joking. I just got off the phone with them. I must warn you, though, it's a bit of a rush schedule. They'd originally signed another model for the job, but she had to drop out at the last minute because she just got LASIK eye surgery done. She didn't realize she can't wear eye makeup for two weeks after. Anyway, they want to do the photo shoot next Tuesday so they can make the October issues."

"Next Tuesday?" That was only four days away.

"Will that be a problem?"

"Yes! I mean, no! Next Tuesday's perfect!"

"Super! I'll be in the office tomorrow morning, catching up on some stuff. Why don't you come by and we can go over the paperwork together? Say, ten o'clock?"

"I'll be there. Ohmigod, Giles, I love you!"

"I'm glad you're pleased, Kamille. And get used to it, because this is just the beginning. Once this ad comes out, my phone's going to be ringing off the hook. Everyone's going to want to use that lovely face of yours."

"Ohmigod! Thank you so much!"

Kamille said good-bye and hung up, almost beside herself with excitement. Her mind raced with a frantic to-do list: total body and face wax; mani-pedi; haircut; facial; a two . . . no, three-day cleanse. No LASIK eye surgery obviously, ha-ha. It was hard to organize her thoughts with so much happening . . . and with so many midori sours in her system.

"What's up? You have to explain this movie to me, I have *no* idea what's going on," Simone said, cranking up the volume.

"Giles got me a modeling job!" Kamille practically screamed.

"Get the fuck out of here."

"I'm shooting a perfume ad for Jeunesse. Isn't that the most awesome news, ever?"

"Definitely. Wow, cheers!" Simone raised her empty glass in the air. "Crap, we need to make another pitcher. Hey, does this mean you get free Jeunesse stuff from now on?"

Simone was obsessed with freebies, which made no sense, since her parents were zillionaires. Or her father was, anyway. He was the owner of the ultrasuccessful Pretty Me cosmetics company. He'd left Simone's mom ages ago and moved to London, and Simone hadn't reunited with him until high school, when he moved back to L.A. Kamille knew she liked getting her revenge on him for the years of neglect: by stealing his new (twenty-four-year-old) wife's designer outfits out of her closet, having sex in them, and returning them stained . . . by marching into Pretty Me salons and demanding thousands of dollars of free products and free services . . . and in general being an attention-whore pain-in-the-ass.

"I don't know if I'm getting free Jeunesse stuff, Simone," Kamille told her. "Anyway, who cares? Ohmigod, I can't believe this is happening! I've gotta tell my mom!"

"Yeah, your mom's totally not a bitch like my mom. My mom would be, like, 'Who'd you blow to get this job?'" Simone picked up Kamille's phone and started scrolling through it. "Your mom'll be superproud of you, though. She'll probably buy you a new car or something."

Kamille blinked. Her mother, proud of her? She couldn't remember the last time. The thing was, Kass was a hard act to follow. She was basically Miss Perfect. Kamille, on the other hand, led a more spontaneous, less OCD life. She was on her way to achieving great, amazing things. But "her way" wasn't the same as Kass's. Kass was all about pros-and-cons lists, schedules, plans. Kamille was about today, going with the flow, seizing opportunities.

"Wait, why do you have Nola Harrison in your contacts list?" Simone said, scrolling. "Do you know what that witch did when she found out I hooked up with her boyfriend? She sent me a Tiffany box in the mail, full of dog shit." She added, "I'm totally deleting her."

"Fine, whatever," Kamille said distractedly.

Simone squinted at Kamille's phone. "Hey, your loser sister texted like half an hour ago. She said she'll be home soon and that her, uh, 'study group' ran late. Study group, is that like an orgy for geeks? Although I doubt Kass ever gets any. She's totally a virgin, right?"

"What?"

"Or a lesbian? Or is she just trying to *look* like a lesbian, with her baggy man shirts and nasty lip mustache and—"

"*Excuse* me?"

Kamille glanced up, startled. With the TV blaring and Simone blabbering, she hadn't heard Kass come through the front door. Kass was standing in the living room doorway, clutching her backpack to her chest. She was glaring at Simone, her hazel eyes furious.

"Hey, nerd, we were just talking about you! Take a load off!" Simone patted the spot next to her on the couch.

"No, thank you. I don't think I should sit that close to you, Simone, I might catch something. Kam, a word?" Kass said coldly.

"Wait, *what* did she just say to me?" Simone huffed at Kamille.

Kamille put her hands over her ears and shook her head. Tonight was her night. She deserved to bask in her news. The last thing she wanted to do was to play referee to Kass and Simone.

"Both of you. Shut up. I want to celebrate," Kamille said irritably.

"Celebrate what?" Kass asked her.

"Her hot British agent just called," Simone said, flipping her long platinum hair over her shoulders. "He got her a big-ass modeling job. For that French perfume company . . . Jeunesse."

"Really?" Kass stared incredulously at Kamille. "Is this true?"

"Of course it's true. What, you think it's a joke?"

"No, no. It's just that . . . oh, never mind! Congratulations!" Kass came over and hugged Kamille.

"Um, thanks."

"We're making more midori sours," Simone told Kass. "You want one, right? Or are you going to wimp out as usual and have a Coke or whatever?"

Kass ignored Simone. "I've gotta go study," she explained to Kamille. "Sorry, big econ quiz on Monday."

"What? Kassie! It's Friday night, and we're celebrating, and . . . look!" Kamille pointed to the TV screen. "It's your favorite scene! Osgood's about to propose to Jerry!"

"I know, I know. TiVo it for me, okay?"

As Kass wandered down the hall to her room, Kamille wondered what was up with her. Sure, she'd walked in on Simone saying bitchy things about her behind her back. But that was Simone being Simone, and Kass must be used to it after all these years. Couldn't she make an exception just this once and hang out with them? Kamille had just gotten the biggest news of her life.

Or was something else bothering Kass?

EIGHT

KYLE

"C AT ON A *HOT TIN ROOF* IS ONE OF TENNESSEE WIL-
liams's most famous plays," Benjy told Kyle. "They made
a movie out of it, too. Have you seen it?"

"Cat on a hot tanned *what*?" Kyle said distractedly.

She lay back on the chaise longue and admired her own
awesome tan. Her legs looked especially stunning against the
pale turquoise color of her new bikini, which she had conve-
niently gotten for free during last Saturday's shoplifting spree
at the mall. Kyle had never shoplifted before, but her friends
Ash and Priscilla had talked her into it. It had been a blast,
like playing an Xbox game, for real. It had also been surpris-
ingly easy, due to the apparent epidemic of brain-dead security
guards.

"*Cat on a Hot Tin Roof*," Benjy repeated. "We have a test on it in our lit class tomorrow. Remember?"

"Oh, yeah." Kyle glanced sideways at Benjy, who was sitting cross-legged on the pool deck surrounded by a sea of notebooks, pens, and books, like some geek in a Staples ad. With his brown eyes and tall, lean frame, he looked a little like Beau, except for his I'm-too-much-of-a-nerd-to-bother-with-my-appearance vibe. His wavy light brown hair was longish and unruly, his gold-rimmed glasses were crooked, and his Korn T-shirt (really? Korn?) and khaki shorts were wrinkled, as though he hadn't quite gotten the hang of laundry yet.

Still, he was cute. Correction: he *would* be cute, if he wasn't her stepbrother.

"You *did* read it, right?" Benjy asked her.

Kyle shrugged nonchalantly. "Can't you just tell me what it's about?"

"Yeah, I'm sure that's what your mom and my dad had in mind when they hired me to be your tutor."

"It'll be our little secret, then."

Kyle still couldn't believe that her mother and Beau had given her an ultimatum: show up for these biweekly tutoring sessions and reach a 3.0 average by the end of the trimester, or she would lose her car, phone, and computer privileges for the entire following trimester. Were they serious, threatening her like that? Unfortunately, there was nothing she could do but go along with their diabolical plan. Or *pretend* to go along with it, anyway, until she could think of a better alternative.

Benjy picked up his dog-eared copy of the play and began leafing through it. "Okay, so, did you read *any* of it?"

"Yeah."

"How far did you get?"

"I don't know. Some girl named Maddy was bitching out some guy named Brett."

"Maggie. And Brick. They were probably having one of their big fights."

"About what?"

"About his drinking. About his messed-up relationship with his dad. About his psycho sister-in-law who's angling for the family fortune. About his dead best friend, Skipper, who may or may not have wanted to hook up with him. Oh, and speaking of sex, they fight a lot about that, too. She hasn't gotten any from him in a *long* time."

Kyle raised her eyebrows. "Why not? The way she looked in that white dress? I totally would have hit that."

"Oh, so you *did* see the movie?"

"Um, maybe?"

Actually, Kyle had read the play last night, cover to cover, and had liked it so much that she had watched the movie on iTunes, staying up till 2 A.M. But she wasn't about to tell Benjy that. It was a lot more fun, making him work for his ten dollars an hour or whatever her Evil-with-a-capital-*E* parental units were paying him.

"And what did you think?" Benjy persisted.

"It was okay. I could have done better, though."

"What do you mean?"

Kyle studied her nails, which were painted different shades of purple and black. "Like the chick who played the sister-in-law? I thought she was too over-the-top with that part. I would have toned it down, been more subtle. Yeah, Tennessee Williams's lines were over-the-top to begin with. But why not play around with them, go deeper, give them some texture?"

"*Really.*" Benjy stared at her with interest. "I didn't know you were into acting."

"Who says I'm into acting?"

"You. The way your voice got all intense just now. And the way you used the word *texture.* You're a closet thespian, Kyle."

"I'm not gay. More like bi. Or bi-curious, anyway."

"*Thespian,* not lesbian. Have you ever considered joining the drama club at school? You should totally check it out, it's awesome."

"Yeah, right. Like I'm going to hang out with you losers and recite Shakespeare or some medieval bullshit."

"Our next production is a new play by a twenty-year-old Chilean writer. It's based on her experiences as a child prostitute in Santiago."

Kyle raised her eyebrows. That didn't sound completely lame. But she wasn't about to give Benjy the satisfaction. "*Booooring,*" she said out loud.

"If you say so."

Yawning, Kyle picked up her phone and pretended to check her messages. As weird as it was, her stupid stepbrother was right about her. She *was* a closet thespian, which she was pretty sure meant a person in the acting profession. From the time she was five or six, when her father began taking her to private screenings of movies he had produced, she had dreamed about becoming an actress someday. Of course, she had never shared this piece of information with anyone, although her father seemed to just *know,* calling her his "little Audrey Hepburn" and clapping the loudest when she was a sunflower in the elementary school play.

Her father. She didn't like thinking about him. It made her too depressed, and besides, it made her want to kill someone. Maybe her mother? So it was best to keep her mind a numb, emotionless blank slate as far as he was concerned, unless she wanted to start something. Which she didn't.

"Yeah, they're kind of looking for someone for the lead right now," Benjy was saying. "It's the young prostitute character who's based on the playwright."

"I think you should go for it," Kyle said lightly. "Some hair extensions, lipstick, the right clothes . . . you'd be perfect!"

"Fuck you. I think I'll tell your mom that you didn't show up today."

"Don't you dare!"

Benjy held up *Cat on a Hot Tin Roof.* "I won't tell if you can describe one of the play's major themes to me. Like, how about the theme of 'mendacity'?"

"Men-*what*?"

But Kyle knew perfectly well what mendacity was. It was something she was very good at.

Not being truthful.

NINE

KAMILLE

"OKAY, BABY GIRL! LET'S HAVE YOU STRETCH ACROSS the bed and prop yourself up on your elbows," Heinrich told Kamille. "Stare straight at the camera. That's it, *perfect*! Now pout your lips! More! Give me *naughty*!"

Kamille pouted her lips and tried to look naughty for the famous German photographer, feeling extremely foolish as she did so. She was starting to ache from posing for so many hours, and in such uncomfortable positions, and with a giant fan blowing her hair this way and that.

Also, she wasn't crazy about wearing so little clothing and so much body oil in front of the entire crew and also her mother. *Especially* her mother. Granted, Kamille wasn't exactly naked. But she might as well be, in her white cotton nightie. And did they have to flatten her boobs with duct tape? Mario, who was the director of the photo shoot, had actually told her that her breasts were *too* big, and that the photos required a look that was more consistent with the name of the perfume, Lolita. (Giles had to explain to her, privately, that Lolita was from a famous novel by a Russian writer named Vladimir Nabokov, in which an old guy became sexually obsessed with a twelve-year-old girl. *Ew?*)

Right now they were shooting in one of the large penthouse suites at the Chateau Marmont, a gorgeous, glamorous hotel on Sunset Boulevard frequented by celebrities. Earlier in the day, they'd shot out in the garden, with Kamille leaning against a flower-covered stone arch . . . then lying on the ground covered by Barbies and rose petals . . . then standing in front of a palm tree, licking an ice cream cone that kept melting and having to be replaced. Kamille had no idea that photo shoots took so long, and were such hard work. She'd always imagined that the whole thing was superquick: get your makeup done, put on some cool clothes, and take pictures for an hour. She couldn't have been more wrong.

Giles was in one corner of the massive bedroom, checking out the photos of Kamille on a computer monitor. Every once in a while he glanced up and gave Kamille a thumbs-up sign. She couldn't believe that their chance encounter at the Coffee Bean & Tea Leaf, less than two weeks ago, had resulted in *this*. The whole thing was beyond amazing, really—a fairy tale come true.

"Um, excuse me, but could somebody cover up my daughter a little?" Kat called out to a random crew member.

"Mom! I'm *fine*!" Kamille said, blushing. She reached back

and tugged at the hem of her nightie, whereupon Heinrich stopped shooting and Mario started yelling and half a dozen assistants swarmed around her, rearranging and powdering and fluffing. *Great.* Why did her mother have to come along today? Kamille was twenty, not two. Besides, she had Giles here to take care of her. She'd wanted Kat to be proud of her and cheer her on from the sidelines—not act all overcontrolling and overprotective.

"Okay, people, let's try this again," Mario ordered. "Heinrich, can you get some shots of her in that chair?"

"Fine. Somebody please move those lights for me." Heinrich pointed to a row of large, boxy lamps, then repositioned his tripod and gazed through the viewfinder. "*Scheisse,* her nose is shiny. Why is her nose shiny? And her breasts got crooked. Where is the damned duct tape?"

As the assistants continued fussing over her, Kamille closed her eyes and wondered how much longer the shoot was going to take. She would kill for a double cheeseburger and fries, screw the calories; she'd basically been living on carrot juice these past few days, trying to get thin for today. Maybe with Kass later tonight, if she wasn't doing anything? Kamille hadn't seen much of her older sister lately, and when she *did* run into her, at home or the restaurant or the family's house, Kass was quiet and preoccupied. Why was she acting like this? *Maybe she got an A-minus on a test,* Kamille thought bitchily.

The photo shoot was finally over at six o'clock. They had been there since seven that morning. The mood in the room lightened immediately as soon as Mario uttered the words "And that's a wrap!" The crew cheered and clapped and buzzed excitedly.

Giles rushed over and hugged her. "Kamille, you were brilliant!"

Kamille beamed. "Really?"

"These photos are exactly what we needed," Mario called out from the computer monitor, where he was in a huddle with Heinrich. "You're a natural, Kamille!"

"Ohmigosh, thank you!"

Kat appeared and thrust a terry-cloth robe at her. "Put this on, doll. How do you feel? Are you okay? Let's get that makeup off your face, and that . . . that . . . *olive oil* off your body. God, you look like a salad. Or a hooker. Just kidding, honey, but *please,* put on this robe."

"*Mom!*"

"The girls here will take care of Kamille, and we can send her on her way," Giles said, smiling reassuringly at Kat. "You should be proud of your daughter; she did a super job today." He turned to Kamille and squeezed her shoulder. "As I mentioned before, this ad is on a rush schedule. It's going to start appearing in magazines in a few weeks—the October issues. And be prepared, because it's going to change your life. You're going to be a star someday, I can feel it!"

"*Really?*" Kamille whispered, feeling dazed.

"Really. Oh, and I almost forgot to tell you . . . I got a call from the Flower Power people today. They want to talk to me about maybe using you for their next campaign."

"No way! Flower Power jeans? I *love* them!"

"So she'll be wearing *clothes* for that one?" Kat inquired hopefully.

Kamille bit her lip to keep from screaming. She was going

to have to chain her mother to her desk or something for all future shoots.

But she wasn't going to let Kat's psychotic personality ruin her good mood. Giles had said she was going to be a star someday. A *star*! She couldn't wait to tell Kass.

If she would stop being PMS long enough to listen, that is. The *real* PMS, not the Psychotic Mom PMS.

TEN

KASS

KASS SLID THE GLASS DOOR CLOSED AND STEPPED OUT into the yard, feeling the dewy grass under her bare feet. The early autumn air was pleasantly cool and fragrant with jasmine. As she lifted her face to the dark sky, a cloud passed, revealing a full moon.

A full moon! Maybe *that* was why she was feeling so blue? But that was an old wives' tale, and Kass didn't believe in such unscientific nonsense.

She plopped down on a green-and-purple Adirondack chair—she'd painted it herself soon after her father died, because green was his favorite color and purple was hers—and hugged her knees to her chest. She could hear the faint chatter and laughter coming from the dining room inside.

Another Sunday Night Dinner. And another not-so-subtle attempt by her mother to fix her up with Mr. Right. Likely, that was what was making her feel so moody and edgy, not the moon.

Tonight, it was Kat's accountant's nephew Dwight, who liked to talk with his mouth full. (*Really* attractive, watching bits of lasagna flying across the table while he pontificated about the merits of Bud versus Heine.) Last week, it was Kat's favorite salesclerk from Saks, who was nice enough but obviously gay. (Could her mom be more clueless?) And before that, there was Pippa's boring, pretentious son, Parker. He and Kass hadn't gotten along when they were five. Why would they get along now?

And could Kamille shut up already about being a supermodel or whatever? Her agent, Giles, had gotten her an early draft of her perfume ad, and she had passed it around at dinner like it was an Oscar or Nobel Prize or something. Granted, the Annie Leibovitz–style shot *was* stunning: Kamille sitting in a blue velvet antique chair, one leg draped provocatively over the armrest, her indigo eyes wide and childlike as she gazed straight on at the camera. The caption simply said: *Innocence in a bottle. Lolita.* Kamille *did* have that perfect combination of sweetness and sensuality.

Still . . . couldn't she handle her good fortune with humility and grace? Instead, she had to go on and on about it . . . and oh, did she happen to mention that a paparazzo had taken a picture of her this morning as she was leaving Giles's office with him? And did she also happen to mention the hot date she had tomorrow night with a hot music producer—okay, music producer's *assistant*—she met at some sick party at the Thompson Hotel that Giles invited her to? *Blah, blah, blah . . .*

"Kassie!"

Kass glanced up, startled. Kamille was walking across the lawn toward her. *Oops.* Hopefully her sister hadn't suddenly developed telepathic abilities.

"I thought you might need this," Kamille said, holding up a bottle of Chardonnay and two glasses.

Kass smiled, relieved. "Thanks, that's nice of you," she said.

Kamille sat down next to her. She poured two glasses and handed one to Kass. "What's wrong, doll? Everyone's worried about you," she said gently.

Kass took a sip. "What do you mean? I'm fine."

"No, you're *not* fine. I'm your sister and your best friend, remember? I know you better than you know yourself."

"Oh, yeah?"

"Yeah. What can I do to help? You wanna talk? Or go out? Or, hey! Maybe we should take a few days off and do a road trip! When was the last time we did that?"

Kass tried to remember. "Santa Barbara, when you dragged me to that spa," she said after a moment. "No, that was in June! It was July, when we went to Vegas for my twenty-first birthday. Mom and Beau were *not* happy that we snuck off without the rest of the family."

"Yeah, I remember. They figured out where we were and surprised us. I think we were a little out of it when they found us."

"Yeah, just a little." Kass winced at the memory of their mother, Beau, Kyle, Benjy, and Bree walking into their suite at the Bellagio—a suite that Kamille had somehow talked the manager into comping them—and finding the two girls semi-passed-out on the floor like a couple of winos. Kass had never been able to handle liquor well, and Kamille had drunk enough for four people.

"It's Mom, isn't it?" Kamille said suddenly.

"What?"

"All those lame guys she's been inviting to the Sunday Night Dinners, trying to hook you up. *That's* what's depressing you. I would be depressed, too."

And you haven't helped with your celebrity princess attitude, Kass thought wryly. "Mom's just being Mom. But yeah, those guys *are* pretty awful," she said out loud.

"Hey, I know!" Kamille reached into her pocket and pulled out her phone. She began typing. "We need to do this ourselves!"

"Do what ourselves?"

Kamille didn't reply. After a moment she held the phone out to Kass. "What do you think of him?"

Kass stared at the screen, at a head shot of an attractive blond guy in a turquoise polo. "Cute, I guess? Who is he?"

"I have no idea!" Kamille giggled.

"*Huh?* Kam, are you wasted?"

"Not yet! Kassie, this is the website for one of those online dating services. We've gotta sign you up so you can meet him—and other guys like him, too!"

Kass shook her head so hard that she spilled half her wine on her skirt. "Oh, no! No *way*! I am *not* doing online dating!" she protested.

"Why not? Would you rather go out with Mr. Beer Gut inside? Oh, and what about Parker Ashton-Gould? Yeah, I could tell you were really into him when he and Pippa came over. The sparks were *flyyyy-ing*!" Kamille waved her hands in the air, cracking up.

Kass made a face. *Grrr.* Why did her sister have to be right? "Fine! *God!* Let me see that phone," she mumbled.

Kamille beamed and scooted her chair closer to Kass's. She scrolled through the website. "Check *him* out. And *him!* Oooh, he's a *hottie!* It says that he's a . . . huh? . . . lin-guis-tics major at UCLA. What in the hell is that? Does that have something to do with linguine?"

"No, you idiot. Linguistics is the study of language. Really? Where does it say that?"

The two girls continued scanning the website. Kamille polished off the rest of the bottle of wine while Kass stuck to what remained of her glass. Still, she must have gotten a wee bit buzzed, because by the time they went back inside, she had let Kamille talk her into signing up for a thirty-day trial membership to Lovematch.com.

Was she nuts? Probably. But it was definitely better than putting up with another Sunday Night Dinner with another Dwight or Parker . . . or worse.

ELEVEN

KAMILE

MILO, LET'S HAVE A SMILE!"

"Who's your new girlfriend, Milo?"

"Hey, honey, aren't you that model?"

Kamille blinked as the paparazzi's cameras flashed brightly in her face, disorienting her. Making her way down the red carpet, she instinctively reached for the arm of Milo Donovan, the model—well, not just any model, but the hunky underwear model whose latest ads, which were *this close* to being porn, were all the rage now—and tried not to wobble on her six-inch stilettos.

Milo jerked around. "I'm sorry, do I know you?" he said under his breath.

"I'm Kamille. Kamille Romero. Giles introduced us like a minute ago."

"Giles who?"

"Your agent and my agent?"

"Oh, right."

"Hey, Milo! How long have you guys been together?" a paparazzo called out.

"How about a kiss?" yet another shouted.

Milo waved at the reporters and hurried into the club, leaving Kamille standing there alone. Okay, that wasn't *too* humiliating. And did the reporters think she was his girlfriend? *Weird*. She headed into the club as well, wishing she had brought a date. Since she'd broken up with Finn (his reaction to Simone's cell-phone pix of him with the red-haired slore had told her everything she needed to know), she hadn't been seeing anyone seriously. But even Kass or Simone would have been better than coming here alone.

Although she hadn't technically come alone. Giles had picked her up in his awesome silver Rolls and brought her to this event, which was a launch party for a new clothing line by the fourteen-year-old daughter of an aging pop star. Kamille had never been to a launch party before. She had barely even known what a launch party was, before Giles.

Really, she owed him so much. In less than six weeks, she had gone from having exactly zero job prospects, unless she counted working at her mom's restaurant, to being a famous model. (Well, maybe more like "on her way to becoming famous.") And in addition to starting a real career and making real money, she was enjoying a total lifestyle upgrade as well, hanging out at fabulous restaurants, fabulous clubs, fabulous parties. She wasn't exactly a fixture in the scene, and she didn't know many celebrities—yet. But she was getting there. It was what she had always dreamed of, ever since her father's death and the subsequent upheaval. Soon Kamille wouldn't have to worry about maxed-out credit cards or having to shop at consignment stores ever again.

Speaking of Giles . . . where was he, anyway? He had introduced her to the completely rude (but insanely hot) Milo out front and then disappeared to take a call, leaving her to trail behind the male model on the red carpet like a stray puppy. Kamille tried to remember if she had ever been on a red carpet before. Maybe just once, when she was three or four, when her father had been nominated for an Oscar. She barely remembered her brief, confusing foray past the noisy gauntlet of reporters as her father held her tightly in his arms. She recalled blinking sleepily at the flashbulbs—she'd skipped her nap that day—and feeling so uncomfortable in her crinkly gold taffeta dress.

Inside the crowded club, Kamille glanced around. The fourteen-year-old fashion designer (it was hard to think of her that way . . . she was *so young*), who was sporting one of her creations (a skintight red maxidress that made her look like a giant LEGO), was gyrating on the dance floor with a dozen drunk teens as a giant clown rode by on a tricycle (WTF?). A waitress in a tank top and thong and nothing else came by and offered Kamille a tray of what looked like raw octopus tentacles. Kamille couldn't say no fast enough. What she really needed was a drink. The bar. Where was the bar?

"Are you lost?"

Kamille turned around at the sound of the friendly male

voice and found herself staring into the most amazing pair of blue eyes, ever. The eyes went with a chiseled jaw, curly blond hair, and big, muscular shoulders. God, who *was* this guy?

"Are you okay? Can I get you anything?" he went on.

Actually, he looked kind of familiar. "Do I . . . know you?" she asked him hesitantly.

"You do now. I'm Chase. Chase Goodall." He held out his hand.

Chase Goodall . . . Chase Goodall . . . And then it came to her.

"You're the baseball player!" Kamille exclaimed. "You play for the Dodgers, right? I've seen you on TV." She'd also seen him in Simone's *Hunks of Major League Baseball* calendar, at her apartment. Simone had made some crass comment once about spending a fun night in with Chase's picture and her favorite dildo. Kamille shook his hand.

Chase grinned. "Guilty. And you've gotta be an actress or a model. You're way too beautiful not to be."

Kamille felt herself blushing. "I just started modeling. My first ad just came out, for this French perfume called Lolita, but you probably don't know it, since you're a guy and all," she babbled.

"Wow, congratulations! Hey, let me get you a drink. What's your poison? Wine? Beer? Appletini?"

"An appletini sounds great, thanks."

Chase put his hand on her elbow and steered her to a nearby booth. The brief contact felt warm. And pleasant. She sat down, and he sat down next to her—not so close as to make her think he was a creeper, but close enough so that she could smell the faint, woodsy aftershave on his skin. Yum.

Within seconds, one of the half-naked waitresses appeared and took their order.

"So who are you?" Chase leaned toward Kamille and stared intently into her eyes.

"Oh! I'm sorry! I'm Kamille Romero."

"Kamille Romero. Are you related to Robbie Romero? Lakers forward?"

"Hmm, not that I know of. But my mom's Kat Romero, she owns Café Romero on Santa Monica. And my stepdad, well, he doesn't have the same last name, but he's Beau LeBlanc, and actually, he used to pitch for—"

"Beau LeBlanc, *seriously?*" Chase cut in. "He's like a legend on our team. Wow, I would love to meet him sometime. How long has he been your stepdad? Is it true he likes to eat steak and mashed potatoes for breakfast?"

Kamille laughed. "Yeah, he's a freak."

"No, it obviously works for him. What's he doing now?"

"He's like semiretired, semi not. He works part-time as a roving instructor for minor league teams, and as a scout for the majors, too. My mom has her restaurant, so Beau helps out a lot with the house and the dogs and the younger kids in our family. My sister Kyle and my stepbrother, Benjy, they're sixteen, and my stepsister, Bree, she's ten."

The waitress returned, practically brushing her massive, jiggly boobs against Chase's face as she bent over and set their drinks on the table. To his credit, he never broke eye contact with Kamille. In general, he seemed oblivious to the wave of rabid female attention radiating his way, not just from the slore server girl but from most of the women in the room.

Of course, Kamille was aware that she was similarly the

object of much of the *male* attention in the room. Much of the *straight* male attention, anyway; the rest of it was going to Chase. Suddenly she realized that the two of them were kind of the "it" couple at this party. Not that they were a couple, but still.

The realization made her feel giddy. And at the same time intensely self-conscious. Like, how obvious was that nasty zit on her forehead? And did she look fat in her new LBD?

She took a sip of her drink. Vodka was an excellent antidote for . . . well, just about anything. "So. How do you like being a baseball player?" she chirped. Okay, so vodka was *not* an excellent antidote for lame getting-to-know-you questions. She took another, much longer sip.

"I love it. I love pitching. Most days, I feel like the luckiest guy on earth. What about you? How do you like modeling?"

"It's still so new," Kamille admitted. "Mostly, it's kind of amazing. I mean, just this summer, I was waitressing at my mom's restaurant and wondering what to do with my life. And then I met Giles—he's my agent—and he got me the Lolita ad. He's trying to line up more jobs for me, too, like this one with Flower Power jeans. And well, of course, I get to go to lots of fun parties. Like this one." She finished off the rest of her appletini. "I've got to admit, though . . . I was so nervous during the Lolita shoot. Like I didn't know what I was doing. That's dumb, right?"

"Nah, I go through that sometimes before a game," Chase said. "When it happens, I find a quiet corner and pray. It totally works."

Kamille started. "You . . . pray?"

"Yeah. My faith is pretty important to me. My parents raised me that way. They're the best."

"Mine, too!"

"Yeah? I'd love to—oh, excuse me, I gotta get this." Chase picked up his cell. "Hello? *What* time's the flight? Oh, sorry, I lost track of the—yeah, I'll be right there." He turned to Kamille. "I really apologize, but I've gotta run. I'm doing this charity thing in Wisconsin tomorrow morning. It's for kids with leukemia. I've gotta be at LAX in, like, twenty minutes."

"Twenty minutes! Ohmigod, go!"

"Not before I get your phone number. That is, if it's okay for me to take you out to lunch sometime."

Lunch, dinner, a trip to Cabo . . . anything. "Sure, that would be great," Kamille said, forcing herself to sound casual versus, say, easy and/or desperate. "It's terrific that you're doing this thing for the kids. And I'm glad we met. It was fun hanging out."

Chase nodded and smiled. "We'll definitely do this again."

As Kamille typed her phone number into his phone, she wondered how she had gotten so lucky. Chase was gorgeous, kind, and thoughtful. And a famous athlete. And he went to church. And he had a close-knit family. And he did charity work for sick children.

There was no question about it. She was in love.

TWELVE

KASS

"YEAH, BEING A ONE-L IS DEFINITELY A CHALLENGE," Mike told Kass. "It's really true what they say. The first year of law school's the toughest. My contracts professor is such a hard-ass, he makes people cry. In class. And not just the girls either."

"That's insane," Kass said, taking a bite of her Yucatán veggie burger. It was Friday at lunchtime, and the outdoor café overlooking South Figueroa Street was packed with USC students. "So what kind of law are you interested in? Litigation? Tax law? That's where all the money is, right?"

"Actually, I want to specialize in international human rights law. There's a lot of bad stuff happening in the world, and I want to help. Money's not a priority for me. I mean, sure, you gotta be able to pay the bills. But I don't need to be a gazillionaire. It's more important for me to give back, make a contribution."

"Really?"

Kass regarded Mike with interest. She had met him through Lovematch.com, the online dating site her crazy sister had convinced her to try, and this was their first date.

So far, so good. Mike was cute (except for the weird mole on his chin, but who was she to be picky?) and supersmart. And he wanted to do human rights work.

In any case, he was certainly better than the other four guys she'd met up with through Lovematch. The first one couldn't stop talking about his ex-girlfriend. The second one wanted to know if Kass could help him score some Vicodin. The third one was married and only interested in NSA (i.e., no-strings-attached). The fourth one explained that he lived with his mother and that the two of them were kind of a package deal (which was *way* too *Psycho*/Norman Bates for Kass's taste).

Mike glanced at his watch and signaled the waitress for a check. "I have to run. I've got torts at one-thirty, and the professor is *not* cool about lateness. So can we do this again? I had a great time."

"Definitely," Kass said, meaning it.

Mike leaned forward and squeezed her hand. "Listen. I like you, and I feel like we have a connection. So before we go out again, there's something I want to tell you about me. Something important."

"Um, sure." Kass wondered what the big secret was. Maybe he was a celebuspawn? Or a closet Republican? As long as he wasn't married, or addicted to pain meds, or . . .

"There's a side of my personality that not many people know about," Mike went on. "I like to wear women's underwear. In fact, I'm wearing some right now. Don't get me wrong, I'm not gay. I'm not even bi. My therapist says it's a very normal expression of my inner femininity. I hope you're cool with that."

It took Kass all of her self-control not to start swearing . . . or cracking up . . . or both. "I'm really happy for you that you're into your, uh, inner femininity," she managed to say after a moment. "It's, uh, kind of a lot for me to digest right now. Can I think about it and call you?" Which really meant, *Can I not think about it and not call you?*

"Yeah, of course!" Mike handed the waitress some money and stood up. "Maybe we can go shopping together at Victoria's Secret sometime! Just kidding!"

"Ha-ha, funny!"

After Mike left, Kass finished off her iced tea and stared moodily at the streetscape, the cars, the people passing by. A guy and a girl had stopped on the sidewalk and were kissing passionately. Ugh. Why was everyone in the world in love except for her?

Kass thought about what just happened with Mike. She would have been even more shocked by his revelation, except that her other Lovematch dates had been disasters, too. Was she ever going to meet Mr. Right? Mike had come so close to being second-date material, only to pull his deep, dark, deal-killer secret out of a hat. Did all guys have deep, dark secrets? Were there any nice, *normal* guys out there?

She reached into her purse for her car keys and was about to get up when she spotted a familiar face across the crowded café patio. Eduardo from her econ class. He was sitting at a table with a girl—no, now he was alone, because the girl was looking kind of pissed off and leaving. Was she his girlfriend? Were they having a fight?

Since the beginning of the semester, when Kass had first met Eduardo, she had seen him in class and had several friendly conversations with him about economic stimulus packages and such. He hadn't repeated his original coffee invitation, though. Kass wondered if he was waiting for her to ask *him* out for coffee. Or maybe he just wasn't interested anymore—especially if he had a girlfriend.

Eduardo glanced up and noticed Kass watching him. She averted her gaze and pretended to be very busy counting the keys on her key chain. *Crap, he thinks I'm stalking him,* she thought.

"Hey!" Eduardo waved and walked up to her table, his backpack slung over one shoulder. He sat down in the chair where Mike had been just a minute ago, in his pink satin G-string or whatever. "How's it going? Did you just get here, or are you on your way out?"

"On my way out. How are you?"

"Good! Well, except for my psycho lunch date."

"Aw, I'm sorry. Girlfriend problems?"

"Girlfriend? No way. She's . . . well, I met her through this dating website. Turns out she's got issues. She got mad at me because I wouldn't meet her psychic to make sure we were meant to be together."

"Seriously?" Kass giggled. "That's so funny, because I just had a bad date, too. With a guy I met through Lovematch .com. He's into—well, never mind. You wouldn't believe it if I told you."

"Try me."

Kass told him. Eduardo raised his eyebrows. "Huh. Well, at least he was honest about it."

"I guess? I'm beginning to think online dating is a big, fat waste of time."

"Yeah, I'm with you there. I think I'd rather hang out with friends."

"Yeah, me, too."

They sat in silence for a moment. Kass gazed at Eduardo. He was so cute. And he seemed like a great guy. What would it hurt for her to ask him out? As friends?

Kass picked up her napkin and folded it into quarters. Then eighths. "So, speaking of hanging out . . . have you seen the new Woody Allen movie?" she said casually.

"No! I've been wanting to check that out."

"Me, too! So do you want to . . . I mean, are you free, like . . . I don't know, maybe this weekend?"

"I'm actually going out of town. My cousin's getting married in Palo Alto. But I'll be back Sunday night. How about then?"

"Sunday night's perfect. As long as it's late-ish, like eight or nine?"

"Late-ish is good. It's a date, then."

"As friends," Kass said with a smile.

"As friends." Eduardo smiled back.

When Kass left the café a few minutes later, she was still smiling. Why was she in such a good mood all of a sudden?

THIRTEEN

KYLE

I DIDN'T KNOW KAMILLE WAS HOOKING UP WITH MILO Donovan," Kyle said, scrolling through the latest issue of *Dish* magazine on her laptop. "God, that's not fair. I wonder if she'd be into sharing?" Just looking at the image of physically perfect Milo made her feel seriously horny.

"Uh, can we please get back to the Civil War? Quiz tomorrow, remember?" Benjy reminded her. He peeked over her shoulder. "Besides, that picture's Photoshopped."

"What the fuck are you talking about?"

Benjy pointed to the photo of Kamille, who was dressed in some skanky-looking black dress and gazing up adoringly at

Milo. "See the edges of her hair? That's a bad pen-tooling job. And see how the two of them are lit differently? The magazine took two separate photos and made it look like Kamille and this dude were standing next to each other."

"How do you know that?"

Benjy grinned. "I'm a genius, I know everything. That's why I'm making the big bucks, being your tutor. Besides, I thought your sister was dating Chase what's-his-name? The baseball player?"

"She's your sister, too. I think Kamille's been on like one date with him. Besides, she's a total slore, she's probably hooking up with both of them."

"I'll tell her you said that."

"Yeah, go ahead."

Bored, Kyle Googled "Kamille Romero," "Milo Donovan," and "Chase" (she couldn't remember his last name). Seconds later, a number of items came up:

MILO'S GIRLFRIEND CHEATS ON HIM WITH BASEBALL PLAYER

MILO: SHE BROKE MY HEART!

SUPERSTAR CHASE GOODALL SMITTEN WITH SOON-TO-BE SUPERMODEL KAMILLE ROMERO

CHASE AND KAMILLE FIGHT ABOUT HIS OTHER GIRLFRIENDS!

MILO'S SECRET GAY PAST

CHASE'S BODYGUARD TELLS ALL!

KAMILLE'S SECRET LESBIAN PAST

KAMILLE PREGNANT WITH CHASE'S BABY!

Kyle read the headlines out loud to Benjy. "Are these magazines allowed to make this shit up? Isn't that illegal or something?" she said incredulously.

"Yeah, and did you notice? They're always quoting a so-called inside source, too, like it's all true."

"Hmm, I think I'll start doing that. You know, writing papers for school and not researching any of it and saying it's all based on 'inside sources.'"

"Good one! Okay, so, back to the important stuff."

"Huh?"

Benjy flipped through his notebook. "Can you tell me who Jeb Stuart was? Was he with the Confederacy or the Union?"

Kyle narrowed her eyes at him. Did he have to be such a buzz kill? Still, he did look kind of cute today in his untucked white button-down, left over from today's school uniform, and distressed jeans. "Can't we do something fun? Hey, you wanna go for a swim?" she said sweetly. She typed in the URL for the weather website, to see what the temperature was like outside.

"No. And you need to stop surfing. Give me that." Benjy reached over, picked up her laptop, and snapped the lid shut.

"Hey, asshole! Give that back!"

"Not until we finish studying for the quiz."

"*No!* Give it *back!*"

Benjy set the laptop on a bookshelf behind him, out of

her reach. She lunged for it, and he blocked her. Furious, she punched him in the stomach, hard.

"*Ow!* What the *hell*?" Benjy yelled. He grabbed her arm and twisted it behind her back. "Fine, you want to play rough? We can play rough."

Actually, that hurt. Kyle squirmed. "Let me go!"

"Not until you apologize for punching me."

"No!"

She tried to free her arm, and they struggled. Benjy hooked his foot around her ankle, knocking her off balance, and she fell to the floor, pulling him down with her. They rolled around and around on the carpet, trying to gain the upper hand, neither one quite succeeding.

All of a sudden Kyle started laughing. Benjy started laughing, too. Then, in the next second, something changed. They stopped laughing, and they stared at each other, breathing hard. Kyle was lying on top of Benjy, and before she could stop herself, she was kissing him, and he was kissing her back. His mouth was hot and delicious, like butterscotch. She could feel his hand under her T-shirt, fumbling awkwardly in the general vicinity of her bra strap.

What in the hell are we doing? Kyle thought wildly. *What if someone walks in? What if Benjy tries to go all the way?* She hadn't made out with that many guys (or girls), even though she liked to pretend that she had, and she was still carrying her V-card around, even though she didn't advertise that fact either. It was an image thing. Mostly, she preferred her solitude. Relationships, even casual hookups, could get so messy and complicated. She really just wanted people to leave her alone.

Except for right now. Making out with Benjy felt so good. Their bodies entangled, their tongues intertwined . . . she could do this all afternoon.

"We should stop," Benjy said suddenly.

"You're right, we should," Kyle agreed.

They kept kissing.

FOURTEEN

KAT

"OHMIGOD! WE'RE HAVING SUNDAY NIGHT DINNER with a famous baseball player!" Bree shrieked. "I have to put this on my Facebook status right this second!" She pulled out her phone and began typing furiously.

"Because we've never had any other famous baseball players in our house before? Thanks, honey," Beau joked.

Chase grinned. "Yeah, the honor's all mine, Mr. LeBlanc. I've always wanted to meet you, and now here I am, in your home, eating this fantastic—what did you call it?" he said, turning to Kat.

"'Spapizza.' Beau invented the recipe. It's part spaghetti with meatballs, part pizza," Kat explained.

"Yeah, it's kinda different, isn't it? And please call me Beau, you're making me feel old."

"You *are* old, Daddy," Bree said without looking up from her phone. "I think you're the oldest dad in my class! Well, except for Savannah's dad, he's like eighty."

Everyone laughed. Kat glanced around the table, happy that people were enjoying themselves (well, *most* of the people, anyway—was something up with Kyle and Benjy?) and feeling warm and relaxed from the lovely Cabernet, courtesy of Chase, who seemed to know how to make the right gestures when "meeting the parents" for the first time.

Yet she was a little anxious, too. About Chase, actually. Kamille had been dating him for exactly two weeks, and she appeared—typical Kamille—to be madly in love, almost ready to walk down the aisle. She and Chase had been holding hands and stealing kisses and giggling at each other's dumb jokes nonstop since arriving at the house. He was everything Kamille had said he was when she first told Kat about their relationship: handsome, charming, considerate. And he seemed pretty crazy about Kamille, too.

Still, Kat couldn't ignore the magazine covers she'd seen in the grocery-store lines, ever since Chase joined the Dodgers and became their resident hottie. They showed him partying at clubs, juggling multiple celebrity girlfriends, and getting caught in alleged "cheating scandals." Was that the real Chase? Or was that just the tabloids distorting the truth to sell copies? Sitting here, he seemed like a great guy, and so attentive to Kamille . . .

. . . who, on the other hand, didn't have the best judgment

when it came to boyfriends. Kamille was always falling in love with the wrong guy and getting her heart broken.

"Chase, let me borrow you for a sec. I want to show you some of my old trophies," Beau said, standing up.

"Seriously? I'd love that, sir! I mean, Beau!" Chase said eagerly.

The two men got up and wandered off to Beau's study. Beau had his arm around Chase's shoulders and was talking animatedly about RBIs and such. Baseball soul mates. Kat studied the remaining faces around the table: Bree, Kass, Kyle, Benjy, and, of course, Kamille, who was staring after Chase like a lovesick teenager. Kass was unusually cheerful; she'd announced earlier that she had to dash after the lemon-cake course because she was seeing a movie with a friend later, saying the word *friend* with a lilt in her voice Kat had never heard before. Could she be going out on an actual *date*? Maybe with Parker Ashton-Gould or one of the other young men Kat had set her up with? It was a nice thought.

Kyle, on the other hand, had been in a weird funk all night—weirder than usual, that is, in that she hadn't said a single bitchy, sarcastic thing to anyone since sitting down. In fact, she had been mysteriously silent, except to say "please" and "thank you" when asking for food to be passed. Kyle, saying "please" and "thank you"? Had she undergone a brain transplant when Kat wasn't looking?

Benjy was his normal subdued self, except that he kept sneaking looks at Kyle across the table and then quickly look-ing away. What was going on between those two? Maybe they were having problems with their tutoring arrangement? Kat made a mental note to speak to Beau about it. They were over-due to check in with Benjy on Kyle's progress, anyway.

After dinner—Kass had said her good-byes and rushed off, Kyle and Benjy had disappeared to their respective rooms, Bree had taken the dogs outside, and Beau and Chase were still holed up in Beau's study having their male-bonding time—Kat found herself alone in the kitchen with Kamille, doing the dishes.

"*Sooooo?*" Kamille said eagerly. "What do you think? Isn't he perfect? He's perfect, right?"

"He seems very nice," Kat replied vaguely. "You guys seem, um, pretty serious."

Kamille beamed and nodded. "We are! Sort of! I mean, we've only been out on a few dates. And we haven't—that is, I mean—well, you know what I mean. Chase is a total gentle-man. He hasn't pressured me to . . . well . . . you *know*. Okay, TMI! But I really like him, Mommy! And I think he likes me, too! He says he wants me to meet his parents sometime. They live in Laguna, that's where he grew up, and he's superclose to them. They go to church as a family, just like we do!"

"Really?" Kat began loading dishes into the dishwasher, buying herself time so she could choose her words carefully. "Honey. I don't mean to sound like an overprotective mom. But I *am* an overprotective mom, we all know that, and I don't want to see you get hurt."

"What do you mean, get hurt?"

"*Welllll* . . . Chase has kind of a reputation."

"Mom! *Seriously?* Have you been reading those stupid tab-loid magazines?" Kamille cried out. "Those stories are completely made up, you know that, right? Like, did you know they're saying Milo Donovan and I are dating? Milo Donovan, yeah, he's that Bill Boxer model. He and I walked into a party together, it was completely random, and because of that, the magazines are calling us a couple. Isn't that insane? Just like those stories about Chase are insane!"

"So . . . you've read them?" Kat asked her.

Kamille shrugged. "Some of them. They're total lies! Chase is such a forgiving person, he's not even mad at those report-ers. He says they have to make a living, too. Anyway, besides, he has a publicist now who handles them. He just hired this woman, Zoe something, she's supposed to be amazing. She's going to start dealing with all those reporters so Chase doesn't have to."

"Uh-huh."

Kamille pouted. "Mommy, please be *happy* for me. Chase is the first perfect guy I've met in . . . well, never. I really like him, and I really want to keep seeing him. So can you just be sweet and supportive and not all worried-mom-like?"

Kat laughed and hugged her. "Okay, doll. I won't be all worried-mom-like."

LATER, AFTER CHASE AND KAMILLE HAD LEFT, AND THE other kids and Coco and Chanel had gone to sleep, Kat turned to Beau as they were brushing their teeth in the his-and-hers, side-by-side bathroom sinks. "So what do you think?" she asked him, her mouth full of toothpaste.

"Of what, darlin'?"

"Chase. What do you think of Chase?"

"Oh! Well! I liked him. I liked him very much. And he's a mighty fine pitcher, too. Really glad he and Kamille are together." Beau grinned. "Was it just me, or do they seem like they're ready to start picking out baby names? They seemed awfully cozy."

"Don't *say* that!"

"Why not? Not ready to be a grandma yet? You'd be the sexiest grandma in the state of California, I tell you that," Beau teased her.

Kat spit out her toothpaste. "No, I'm not ready to be a grandma! And Kamille's not ready to be a mom! Or a wife! She's only twenty years old. Besides, I'm not so sure about Chase. I think he's a player, not a settling-down type."

"Yeah, he's a player. He's a *baseball* player. You know, not every good-looking guy is a—what's that term the kids use?—*man-whore*. Look at me!" Beau wiggled his eyebrows.

"Ha-ha, very funny."

"I'm completely devoted to you. And from the looks of it, Chase seems pretty devoted to our Kamille."

Kat didn't reply. She hoped, sincerely hoped, that Beau was right. But she couldn't shake the nagging feeling that Chase's tabloid image might not be so far from reality.

Or was she just being too "worried-mom-like"?

FIFTEEN

KAMILLE

So . . . welcome to my place," Chase said as he ushered Kamille through the front door. "Let me take your coat."

Kamille paused in the terra-cotta-tiled foyer and shrugged off her faux-mink jacket for Chase. She glanced around, excited to finally see his house, which was nestled on a secluded lot in exclusive Holmby Hills.

He had suggested that they stop by for a nightcap after the Sunday Night Dinner, and even though she was tired, she'd said yes. She hadn't wanted the evening to end just yet. The dinner had gone so well; everyone seemed to love Chase . . .

. . . except for her mom, who could be Ms. Judgmental when it came to Kamille's boyfriends. Of course, Chase wasn't just any boyfriend, and Kat would come around. Eventually. In the meantime, Kamille wasn't going to let that stressful little mother-daughter talk ruin her good mood.

At least I have *a boyfriend,* Kamille thought smugly. Although Kass had said something about meeting up with some guy named Eduardo later tonight? So maybe there was hope for her, after all.

"What do you think? It's not too much of a grungy bachelor pad, is it?" Chase joked as they headed into the living room.

"Ohmigosh, no! It's incredible!" Kamille gushed. She glanced around the room, at the blue and yellow walls and the mix of wicker and hand-painted Mexican furniture. "Did you decorate it yourself? It's so pretty! Well, not 'pretty,' but whatever the guy version of 'pretty' is. You know what I mean, right?"

"Yeah, I know what you mean. And no, I hired a decorator to do it. I told her I wanted it to look kind of like my parents' house, the house I grew up in. That explains why it's kind of beachy looking. I wanted a lot of family photos on the walls, too. See, that's me when I was five." Chase pointed to a framed picture on top of a white baby-grand piano.

Kamille walked over to take a closer look. Chase at five was an adorable boy with a headful of floppy blond curls. In the picture, he was holding up a toy sailboat and grinning proudly.

"You're so cute!" Kamille told him.

"Yeah, actually, I was kind of a handful. My mom'll tell you. And over there on the wall . . . that's her and my dad. The two guys with surfboards, those're my brothers, Zach and Justin. Zach's at UCLA—he's a business major—and Justin's a senior in high school. And the girl on the mountain bike, that's my sister, Amanda. She and Justin are twins."

"You have a big family!"

"Yeah, just like you." He smiled and added, "That's what I want, too, someday. A lot of kids."

"Yeah, me, too."

For a moment Kamille imagined her and Chase getting married and starting their own family. The thought made her blush furiously, and she turned away, hoping Chase didn't notice. She busied herself scrutinizing the rest of his family photos.

Chase came up behind her. He wrapped his arms around her waist and kissed the top of her head. The kiss felt so tender that Kamille knew, in that instant, that Chase had the same fantasy, too, of marriage and kids. With her. The thought made her weak in the knees.

"Kamille." Chase turned her around and stared into her eyes. "I know this is all moving kinda fast, but . . . do you believe in love at first sight?"

"Do I . . ."

Kamille hesitated. How could she explain this to him? Of course she believed in love at first sight. She was the queen (or rather, princess) of love at first sight. But with all her other boyfriends, she only *thought* she was in love. She knew now that those were just dumb crushes (at best) or dysfunctional dramas (at worst), like the times she would fall for guys who treated her like dirt, and then continue falling deeper the worse they treated her. How messed up was that?

But Chase was different. *He* was the one. *This* was what love, and love at first sight, were supposed to feel like. Not pain and rejection and emptiness, but warmth and safety and passion all wrapped up in one amazing package.

Kamille met his gaze, feeling as if her heart were about to

burst out of her chest. She opened her mouth to speak, to tell him all this, to tell him she loved him. But before she could say a word, he put his finger on her lips and whispered, "I want you to come with me."

"Where?"

Without speaking, Chase took her hand and led her to his bedroom. He paused by the terrace door—the view of the city twinkling in the distance was stunning, especially with the pale moon—and wrapped her in his arms. He kissed her, at first gently, and then more urgently. She returned the kiss with the same urgency, knowing at this moment that she was ready to give herself to him completely.

She stepped back and slipped out of her dress, relishing the way his eyes seemed to devour her body. But standing there in her white lace bra and panties and nothing else, she suddenly felt shy. She crossed her arms over her chest.

"Don't do that. I have to look at you. Oh my God, you are the most beautiful thing I have ever seen," Chase murmured huskily.

"I am?"

"I don't think you realize the power you have over men. Over me."

"I don't want to have power over other men. Just you."

"Come here."

They fell to the bed, kissing, caressing each other, peeling away each other's clothes.

AFTERWARD, KAMILLE LAY IN BED AS CHASE TOOK A shower in the adjoining bathroom. Moonlight fell across the room, casting a dreamy silvery glow. She drew the luxurious Egyptian sheets up to her neck and sighed happily. Every cell in her body seemed to hum and vibrate with relaxation, pleasure, bliss.

Now she understood why sex was such a big deal. Her lovers before Chase had obviously been total amateurs. With Chase, she had reached heights she had never dreamed possible. She'd never had an orgasm with a guy, but with Chase . . . well, she had pretty much lost count after the fourth or fifth one.

She closed her eyes and sank down on the impossibly soft pillow. She was exhausted after their lovemaking marathon, and yet, incredibly, she wanted him again. Had she turned into a complete sex maniac? She giggled and buried herself more deeply under the sheets, breathing in the smell of his skin and cologne and their mingled sweat. She felt dizzy with lust and love and a million emotions she had never truly experienced before.

A phone began ringing, interrupting her postcoital coma. She poked her head out. It was Chase's cell on the nightstand. It stopped after six rings, then started up again.

Kamille frowned, annoyed. Who was so eager to reach him, and at this late hour? The alarm clock said 12:24. Curious, she propped herself up on her elbows and glanced at the caller-ID screen.

It flashed: TIFFANI CALLING.

It was like a sucker punch to the stomach. Who in the hell was Tiffani, and why was she calling Chase after midnight? Was she an ex-girlfriend?

For an irrational split second, Kamille contemplated answering the phone. But that would be insane. If Chase walked in on her doing something like that, he might think twice about their relationship. The truth was, she didn't handle jealousy too well. Last year, she had actually found a way to hack into a boyfriend's voice mail because he kept getting calls from a particular number. The person turned out to be his mother. It was not a side of her she wanted to share with Chase—not yet, anyway. Maybe when they'd been together, and she felt more secure with him.

Still, who was this bitch Tiffani?

"Is that your phone? Or mine?"

Kamille jerked her head up and saw Chase standing in the doorway of his bathroom, wearing nothing but a white towel. His hair was damp, and his tanned, rock-hard muscles glistened with moisture. She would have been totally turned on at the sight of him, except that she was distracted by the still-ringing phone. And by the realization that Chase may have seen her checking out the screen, trying to figure out the caller's identity.

"I think it's yours?" Kamille replied casually. "Mine's in my purse."

Chase sauntered over and peered at the screen. His face darkened with annoyance.

"Chase? What is it?"

"It's this girl Tiffani, she's a friend of mine. She's married to one of the guys on the team. I think they're having problems, and . . . uh . . . she calls me a lot to check up on him, ask me if he's with me and stuff. I don't want to get involved, if you know what I mean?"

Relief coursed through Kamille. Why had she been so

paranoid? "I totally know what you mean," she said, smiling sympathetically.

"Yeah, that relationship's a time bomb. She's the most jealous person I've ever met. He's totally not cheating on her, as far as I know, but if he did, I almost wouldn't blame him. She's constantly nagging him about where he's going and where he's been. She even stalks him through his Twitter page. It's like she wants to keep him in a cage."

"Wow, that sounds awful!" Of course, Kamille didn't mention that Twitter-stalking was one of her own tried-and-true strategies.

"It is. But I don't want to talk about them anymore."

Chase turned off his cell and tossed it on the floor. He slid into bed, letting his towel fall away, his eyes blazing with desire as he took in the sight of Kamille's naked body. She gasped when she saw that he was ready to make love to her, again. But why was she so surprised? She wanted him, too. So much.

They didn't go to sleep until the sun came up.

SIXTEEN

KASS

CAN'T BELIEVE I LET YOU TALK ME INTO SEEING A CHICK flick," Eduardo joked as he and Kass walked out of the movie theater at the Grove shopping center. It was Saturday night, and the place was jam-packed.

"Yeah, well, last time it was that postapocalyptic thriller with naked green space-alien women. So I figured it was only fair," Kass joked back.

He laughed and draped his arm around her shoulders. The gesture was casual, but simultaneously not casual. In the last few weeks, Kass and Eduardo had entered that gray area, the one between "just friends" and "something more." They'd been on three outings—Kass refused to think of them as dates— and each time, she liked him more and more.

And he seemed to feel the same. Last weekend, he'd almost kissed her after smoothies at Dlush. But she'd balked, bending down to tie her shoe (which didn't need tying) . . . and the moment had passed, and she'd started babbling awkwardly about Professor Mueller's recent lecture on economic indicators. Eduardo must think she was crazy.

What did she want, anyway? Hadn't she signed up for Lovematch.com to find a love match? Wasn't Eduardo a prime candidate? He was cute, supersmart, sweet, and funny. They liked so many of the same things—not just movies and high finance but obscure novels, politics, the Food Network, and old TV shows.

And it wasn't as though she wasn't attracted to him. She was, big-time. She'd even had a dream about him the other night that was seriously X-rated, involving handcuffs and a Nordstrom dressing room and—

"Hey, Earth to Kass. Are you hungry? I know a great taco stand at the Farmers Market." Eduardo was smiling at her curiously.

"What? Oh, sure!"

"Awesome. Tacos, it is, then."

They strolled slowly past the lit-up fountain in the middle of the plaza, which Kass had always loved. Her father used to bring the three girls to the Grove a lot—especially during the holidays, to catch the big tree and the fake snow falling at night. He always made sure to get in line with the other parents to see Santa, who held court for all the spoiled brats dressed in their Armani Baby and Ralph Lauren outfits.

Christmas was coming up in a couple of months. Another Christmas without him.

Kass sighed heavily.

"You okay?" Eduardo asked her.

She instinctively nestled into the crook of his arm. "Yeah. Just hungry, I guess."

"We'd better feed you right away, then."

They headed over to the Farmers Market next door. The Farmers Market was another one of Kass's favorite spots in L.A. There were dozens of food stands under one roof, everything from Korean barbecue to French crêpes.

Eduardo led her to the taco stand and ordered for both of them. "Fish tacos, chips, *pico de gallo,* and a couple of Coronas. Is that okay with you?"

"Sounds perfect."

When they got their food, they sat down at a rickety metal table. The place was packed, with the usual mixed crowd of couples, families with small kids, college students, tourists, and senior citizens. From the other end of the market, Kass could hear the faint strains of a live band playing zydeco music.

"So." Eduardo squeezed a lime wedge into his beer and took a sip. "I was thinking of driving to San Diego next Saturday, Sunday. There's this new film festival going on, and my friend has a documentary in it."

"Oh? That sounds cool. I'm sure you'll have fun."

Eduardo grinned. "I was thinking that you might come with me."

"Oh!"

Kass picked up her fish taco and bit into it. It was delicious, or it would be, except that she suddenly couldn't taste the food because her mind was racing with this new development. Eduardo was asking her to go to San Diego with him. For the whole weekend. Did that mean he was escalating their "just friends" status? Would they be sharing a room? And if they were sharing a room, did that mean . . .

"I . . . hmm . . . well . . . it sounds amazing," Kass said finally. "I'll have to check with my mom about my schedule at the restaurant, though. And I have this killer paper due for Professor Nazari week after next, and I haven't even started on it."

Eduardo gazed at her thoughtfully. "Okay. Just let me know. And . . . Kass?"

"Yes?"

"Look, I don't want to pressure you. But you know how I feel about you."

I do? Kass thought. And then she remembered that he *had* tried to kiss her last week.

"Maybe you and I want different things," Eduardo went on. "I like hanging out with you. But I kind of want more. Do you know what I mean?"

"Mmm."

"*So.* Anyway, think about San Diego and let me know."

"I will. Hey, did you catch *Top Chef* the other night? Was that Elimination Challenge insane or what?"

As Kass rambled on about *Top Chef,* she was vaguely aware of Eduardo's eyes flicking across her face, her long light brown hair, her tighter-than-usual black T-shirt. (Had she washed it in the wrong temperature?) His look was charged with long-ing, which made her feel kind of warm and tingly, if she had to be honest. But his look was a little sad, too, and mystified, like he was wondering why they weren't at his place or hers right now, getting naked and doing all sorts of unmentionable things.

Blushing, Kass dropped her gaze to the table and busied herself with the *pico de gallo.*

WHEN KASS GOT HOME THAT NIGHT, KAMILLE WAS IN the living room, dancing to Madonna's "Express Yourself." She was wearing nothing but a red baby-doll nightie and leopard-print mule slippers.

"Ohmigod, where's Ballboy? Am I interrupting some weird mating ritual?" Kass said, dropping her backpack and keys on the couch.

Kamille giggled. "He's out with his friends. And stop calling him Ballboy!"

"Okay, so you're practicing to be a stripper. Are the modeling gigs drying up already?"

"You are *such* a bitch. Shut *up!*" Kamille picked up a silk pillow and flung it at Kass.

Kass ducked, laughing. "I've got some leftover tacos. Want some?"

"I had a salad. Giles said I have to watch my weight."

"Why? He's an idiot, Kam, you're perfect!"

"Not really. Hey, you want a drink? I think we have a bottle of white wine in the fridge."

Kass plopped down on the couch and leafed through a stack of unopened mail. "No, thanks. I had a beer tonight. One's my limit, you know that."

"Wuss." Kamille sat down on the couch next to Kass and put her head on her shoulder. "Kassie?"

"What?"

"What do you think of Chase? Honestly? You've met him a bunch of times now. But you haven't said a word about him."

Kass hesitated. She had seen Chase on exactly three occasions: twice at a Sunday Night Dinner, and once, when Kamille had brought him to Café Romero. There was no doubt that he was very charming and very, very hot.

But. She'd caught him checking out one of the waitresses at the restaurant when Kamille was in the ladies' room. And she knew about his tabloid reputation because Kyle had gleefully filled her in. (That girl seriously needed to get off the Internet and get a life.)

Or was Kass being unfair? Maybe she'd misinterpreted that look he gave the waitress? And tabloids weren't exactly a reliable source of information.

It was also possible that Kass was suffering from a huge case of sour grapes. Kamille's modeling career was blossoming. She had a famous boyfriend whom she seemed to really like. Kass, on the other hand, was all about work, work, work—and unable to move forward in her relationship with a great guy, for whatever reason.

Kamille was waiting for an answer. "I like Chase. He's fine," Kass replied vaguely.

Kamille frowned. "*Fine?* Yeah, that's like when you say something tastes 'interesting.' What you really mean is, you don't like him!"

"That's not what I—"

"What is *wrong* with you?" Kamille said, suddenly angry.

"And Mommy, too? Chase is the most amazing guy, ever! Don't you two get it? He's the love of my life, and when we get married, I want him to feel—"

"Wait, *what*? When did you get engaged?"

"We're not engaged. Not yet. But we're in love, and I know he's the one, and I want you all to accept him as part of the family."

"Kam, are you nuts? You've been dating for all of what? A month? Or not even?"

"What difference does it make? A week, a month, a year, ten years . . . when you know, you know! Besides, who are you to talk? How are things going with *your* new boyfriend, what's-his-name, Eduardo? The one none of us has met?"

"That's because he's not my boyfriend. We're just, uh, hanging out."

"Have you guys hooked up?"

"Um . . . no."

Kamille's expression softened. "Do you *want* to hook up?"

Kass hesitated. "I'm not sure," she said after a moment. "I mean, I do. It's just that . . . what if we go there, and then he dumps me? What if he's one of those guys?"

"Okay, time out." Kamille put her hands on Kass's shoulders. "Sweetie, you've had, like, one serious boyfriend your whole life. And you're twenty-one years old. So Adam Kerrigan dumped you senior year of high school—"

"The day after I finally gave it up for him."

"—the day after you finally gave it up for him. He was a douche bag. But not every guy is a douche bag. Why don't you give Eduardo a chance? He sounds supernice, from the, like, one time you told me about him."

"Yeah?"

"Yeah."

"I don't know. I'll think about it."

"Yeah, well, don't spend too many years analyzing the situation like you always do, or you might die a virgin."

"I am *not* a virgin, I just told you, Adam Kerrigan and I—"

"Whatever. Your chastity belt is on so tight, you might as well *be* a virgin. I'm not saying that to be a bitch. I'm saying that because I love you, and I want you to be as happy as I am with Chase."

Kamille reached over and hugged Kass. Kass hugged her back. Was Kamille right? Did she, Kass, need to loosen up a little and let Eduardo score a home run with her?

Or at least get to first base?

SEVENTEEN

KYLE

"SO YOU'RE GOING TO THE PARTY TONIGHT, RIGHT?" Ash called out to Kyle.

"What party?" Kyle slid past Ash and Priscilla and opened her overflowing locker. She nudged a pile of textbooks, note-books, makeup containers, empty Four Loko bottles, and a broken calculator with her foot, trying to stuff everything back inside. She really needed to do a cleanup one of these days. Even her prized pictures of Channing Tatum (shirtless) and Megan Fox (almost shirtless) were ripped and sadly peeling from the locker walls.

Ash and Priscilla exchanged a glance. "At Graydon's," Ash said, running a hand through her short, spiky hair. She dyed it a different color every week. This week, it was fuchsia. "Gray-don Garrison? He's a senior? His parents are in Prague or Ibiza or wherever."

"I went to one of his parties once," Priscilla added. "I hooked up with these two rich Russian guys. They were *so* old, like thirty? They thought I was a ho, and gave me like five hundred dollars afterward." She twirled her long, straight-out-of-a-bottle platinum hair around her finger and giggled.

"I was at that party, too. It was sick. Everyone was doing coke and E. And whippits," Ash added.

"Those skinny little dogs?" Kyle said, confused.

"No, retard. Cans filled with that gas, nitrous something. You put it in balloons and inhale," Ash clarified. "God, are you totally out of it?"

"Where have you been lately, anyway? You haven't gone out with us in, like, forever." Priscilla pouted.

"My parents are making me do like six hours of homework every night. I have to improve my GPA or they're going to send me to a convent," Kyle explained. She knew she was kind of exaggerating with the "six hours" and "convent" part. But that was the only kind of talk Ash and Priscilla understood, especially when they were stoned out of their minds. Which they obviously were, judging from the bloodshot eyes and the smell wafting from their matching white blouses and green-and-black-plaid skirts, aka the suck-ass school uniform.

"Bummer," Priscilla sympathized.

"Yeah, bummer. Hey, isn't that your brother?" Ash said suddenly.

Kyle glanced over her shoulder. Benjy was walking down

the hall with a couple of guys from their literature class, Colt Reichert and Javier something.

"He's not my brother," Kyle said irritably.

Ash shrugged. "Step, half, whatever. He's kind of hot. Like that dude who's really Batman when he takes off his glasses."

"You mean Superman," Kyle corrected her.

"Same difference. You wouldn't mind if I hit that, would you?" Ash puckered her lips and blew a loud kiss at Benjy.

But Benjy didn't seem to notice. He was looking at Kyle.

Kyle turned away, feeling confused and pissed off at the same time. She had managed to ignore Benjy successfully since That Day, and she wasn't about to change that now.

That Day. They had made out for a while, almost going all the way, then stopped at the last minute when Kyle had suddenly freaked out and stormed off without a word. He had texted her later, apologizing and asking if they could talk. She had texted back, saying that she didn't want to talk and didn't want to continue the tutoring sessions with him, and if he had any ideas about narking her out to the parents, she would kill him. He'd never responded, but she hadn't gotten chewed out by Kat and Beau either, so he was obviously complying.

Problem was . . . it meant she actually had to study and do her homework all on her own, so she could reach-slash-maintain a 3.0 average and make it *look* as though Benjy were still tutoring her. *God.* Of course, it wasn't that hard for her to get decent grades. Her classes were actually a piece of cake. It was the principle of it, though. She hated her school, and the idea of school in general. She hated having to follow other people's rules and expectations of who she was supposed to be. An obedient, good-girl, straight-A student? That wasn't her. Okay, so maybe she wasn't the opposite of that either, not entirely. But she felt she had to be that badass rebel, just to broadcast loud and clear to her teachers, parents, society, *everyone*, that she was her own person.

As for Benjy . . . well, the whole thing was just too weird to even process. To be honest, she had *liked* making out with him. But that was demented, right? And maybe even illegal? As in, incest? All she knew was, her mother and Beau would totally lose their shit if they found out. They might even send her to a convent, after all . . . no exaggeration there. She enjoyed pissing off her mother, but not *that* much.

Suddenly in a foul mood, Kyle glared at the photos of Channing Tatum and Megan Fox stuck on the back of her locker door and tore them down. She crumpled them up into angry little balls and tossed them over her shoulder.

They hit some random girl in the head. "What the fuck?" the girl cried out.

"What's the matter with you, Kyle? Channing and Meggie not doing it for you anymore?" Ash teased her.

"Hey, speaking of . . . have you seen the new dude who just transferred here? From New York? He could be Channing's twin," Priscilla gushed.

Ash raised her hand. "Dibs!"

"I called it first! Or, hey, maybe we could three-sixty-nine him . . ."

"I'm late for history," Kyle said, slamming her locker shut. "Later, bitches." She slung her backpack over her shoulder and started down the hall.

"What about tonight? Graydon's party? You want us to pick you up?" Ash called out after her.

"I don't know. Sure. Let me think about it," Kyle replied.

Maybe an out-of-control party was just what she needed to sort out her bad mood and put things in perspective?

EIGHTEEN

KAMILLE

K AMILLE, BLOW A KISSY FACE!"
"Can you two stand closer?"

Kamille snuggled against Chase and smiled for the cameras. They were walking the red carpet at a new club downtown where they were attending a charity fashion show.

They had been dating for a whole month now, but this was only their second public appearance at an event. Chase preferred to go to one of their favorite little restaurants in West Hollywood or Beverly Hills, where the (well-tipped) maître d's helped to shield them from paparazzi, or to stay in.

Mostly, Chase preferred to stay in. In bed. Which was just fine with Kamille. Lately, they had gotten into the habit of ordering in, and making love, and drinking lots of champagne, and making love, and watching old movies or sports games on his giant plasma screen, and making love. It was heaven.

Really, her life was so perfect now. She and Chase were blissfully happy together. The Lolita perfume ad was getting a lot of attention, and she had just started shooting the Flower Power jeans ad today. *Glamour* magazine had interviewed her as part of an article on up-and-coming new faces in Hollywood.

She had been mentioned in other magazines and in the blogs, too—some of it was positive, some of it was not so positive (did that blogger really have to call her fat just because she had curves?), but who was she to be picky? It was all good. Giles had told her that by this time next year, with hard work and luck, she could be right up there with Gisele and Heidi.

"Hey, Chase? Care to make a comment about what happened at Industry last night?" one of the cameramen called out suddenly.

Kamille felt Chase's entire body go tense. She turned to him slightly and whispered, "Industry? What's he talking about?"

"Let's go inside."

"What?"

"I'll tell you when we're alone. *Let's go.*"

Kamille had never heard his voice take on that cold, hard edge. It was all she could do to keep smiling as she blew a kiss at the line of reporters and cameramen and headed into the club, clutching Chase's hand.

Inside, the fashion show was in full force. The rap artist Atomic was acting as MC as various models paraded down the catwalk, dressed in funky resort wear. Kamille recognized several other celebrities in the crowd: more pop stars, actors, other models. She would have enjoyed meeting them and also checking out the fashions, except that Chase was dragging her away from the main room, toward the bar. Something was definitely wrong.

At the bar, he ordered two drinks: a Scotch on the rocks for himself and a glass of white wine for her. Then he picked up the drinks and nudged Kamille into a dark, quiet corner, out of the other guests' earshot.

He downed his Scotch in one gulp, some of it spilling on his beautiful blue Zegna suit. Kamille stared at him, alarmed. She had never seen him like this. "What is it, Chase? What's going on?" she whispered.

"Fucking reporters," Chase burst out. He lowered his voice. "Zoe, my publicist, called me about it this morning. Some tabloid sleazebag took a picture of me at Industry last night."

Kamille felt her blood go cold. "What . . . picture? I thought you were out with your teammates."

"I was. Thing is, we got a little drunk. You know, typical boys' night. I had this breakfast thing at seven A.M. sharp, though, so I got up to leave. *Alone,* mind you. So I'm at the valet waiting for my car, and this girl comes out of nowhere. Next thing I knew, she's got her hands all over me and she's insisting I go back to her place with her. I tell her no, thanks, but she won't back off. I think she was high on something. I finally had to say some pretty nasty stuff to her, and she got the message. But not before some asshole reporter takes a picture."

"I don't understand. How bad can it be? It's just some random fan-girl attacking you, right? You must get that a lot."

"Yeah, but the picture could be . . . open to misinterpretation."

Misinterpretation? "So you've seen it?"

"Zoe texted it to me. 'Sides, it's on the fucking Internet now."

This was all news to Kamille. She had been holed up at a shoot all day and hadn't been online. And why was Chase swearing so much? It wasn't like him. "Can I see it?" she said out loud.

"What?"

"The picture. Can I see it?"

Chase sighed. "Fine. You're gonna see it eventually, anyway."

He pulled his phone out of his jacket pocket and scrolled around. After a moment he held up the screen for her to look. "Here. Satisfied?" he grumbled.

Kamille squinted to see in the dim light. She took the phone from him and enhanced the image.

The picture showed Chase with some petite blonde in a black minidress that revealed way more skin than not. Slore couture. Her arms were snaked around his neck, and her head was tipped up to his.

The thing was . . . he wasn't exactly pushing her away. His arms were wrapped around her waist. And his head was bent down low, as if he was a millisecond away from kissing her.

The headline read:

CHASE HOOKS UP WITH FAN AT L.A. CLUB (KAMILLE: "WE'RE THROUGH!")

Kamille realized that her hand was shaking. In fact, she was shaking all over. "What the fuck, Chase?" she cried out. Now *she* was the one who was swearing.

"I told you, Kamille. Goddamned reporters, they make this shit up."

"But, this picture! You're practically making out with her!"

"You ever heard of Photoshopping? Jesus, I can't believe you're buying this."

"Photoshopping?"

"Yeah. They use computers to manipulate pictures. Didn't they do that to you and that Bill Boxer dude, what's-his-name, Miles?"

"I know what Photoshopping is. And it's Milo."

"Yeah, Milo. The magazines were running stories about you guys for weeks, saying you were together. Was *that* the truth?"

"No."

"So why are you taking their side now? After all the crap the tabloids have been saying about me for months. For years!"

"I'm not taking *anyone's* side! God, why are you putting words into my mouth?"

"You said it, not me."

Kamille balled up her fists, feeling *this* close to bursting into tears. But why was she so upset? Chase was right. The tabloids *had* made up that stuff about her and Milo. And she had always believed Chase when he said those stories about him, from before they were dating and even the recent ones, too, were garbage.

So why was she having doubts now? Was it because he was acting so . . . angry? And self-righteous? Like he had something to hide?

"I need another drink. You want one?" Chase started for the bar.

"No. I want to go home."

"What? We just got here."

"I want to go! The night's ruined, and besides, I have a splitting headache," Kamille snapped.

"Jeez, why are you mad at me? I didn't *do* anything."

"Whatever. I'm going home. If you want to stay, fine. I'm sure there are plenty of fan-girls here you can hook up with," she said before she could stop herself.

"Yeah? Fuck you!"

"Fuck *you*!"

Kamille felt as though her head were going to explode. She threw her glass of wine in his face and stormed off. As she passed the bar, she saw two girls gaping at her.

"Ohmigod, did you see that?" one of them said.

The other one held up her cell. "I got a picture! That's Chase Goodall and his new girlfriend. That model, Kathy something. I read about her in *Glamour*. I'm totally Tweeting this."

"Totally!"

Kamille had to fight the impulse to grab the bitch's cell out of her greedy little hand and smash it against the wall. Instead, she began running, and kept running, out of the club and past the red carpet, the line of paparazzi. The fucking paparazzi. She heard the cameras snapping away behind her.

"Kamille, how 'bout a comment on the picture?" one of them shouted.

"Are you and Chase breaking up?" another one added.

The November night had turned chilly. Shivering in her thin silk wrap, Kamille remembered suddenly that Chase had driven them to the party. She glanced around frantically and spotted a black Town Car parked halfway down the block, its engine idling. She hurried toward it, opened the back door, and slid in.

The driver whirled around. "Hey, what are you doing?"

"I'll pay you two hundred dollars to drive me home," Kamille said breathlessly. "It's not far from here."

"What? I'm supposed to wait for my client."

"*Three* hundred. Just drive. *Please!*"

The driver sighed. Then he turned around and pulled into the street.

KAMILLE WASN'T SURE WHAT TIME IT WAS WHEN THE doorbell rang. She glanced up at the alarm clock—was it midnight already? Where was Kass? Oh, right. She had mentioned that she was closing up at the restaurant tonight.

Kamille tried to prop herself up on her elbows and climb out of bed. Her head hurt. Everything hurt. And where did that half-empty bottle of vodka come from? Oh, yeah, she'd poured herself a drink (or maybe several drinks) after the nice driver dropped her off . . .

Staggering to her feet, she saw that she was still wearing her sapphire-blue Valentino dress, which she'd rented for the night. It was badly wrinkled, and there was a stain on the bodice from the wine she'd thrown at Chase.

"Shit," she muttered. "Shit, shit, shit."

The doorbell rang again. Kamille hobbled into the hallway. She had one Louis Vuitton satin mule on, one off. Had she left it somewhere, like Cinderella? She'd better find it, since the shoes, too, were rented. She was making good money these days, but not good enough to buy the major labels. Not yet.

"Who is it?" she called out.

"It's me, Chase. Babe, I need to talk to you."

Hot rage welled up in her chest. She never wanted to see Chase again, ever. "Go away!" she shouted.

"Please. I'm so sorry. Just let me talk to you for a minute, okay? One minute."

Kamille hesitated. Then she unlocked the dead bolt and opened the door.

Chase was standing there, holding a massive bouquet of cream-colored roses. Their perfume filled the air between them, heavy and sweet. She glanced up at his face, at the tears trickling down his cheeks. Ohmigod, he was crying! She had never seen him cry.

"Chase!"

"Kamille, let me talk. I was so wrong to yell at you like that, at the club. I've been under a lot of pressure with the team. My pitching wasn't a hundred percent this season. I want to make sure they renew my contract instead of trading me away. I want to stay in L.A., I want to stay with you." He shook his head. "And this tabloid crap, it's really been weighing on me. It's like they're trying to destroy my reputation, and there's not a damned thing I can do about it. Zoe's working on a counterstrategy, but she's not a miracle worker, you know? I'm a good person, an honest person, I just wanna live my life and be the best ballplayer I can be. And, most important of all, I wanna be with you. Forever and ever. If I lost you over this, or over anything, I couldn't go on living."

Kamille melted. "Oh, Chase."

"Kamille." He rushed in and clasped her fiercely in his arms, crushing the roses between them.

She took them and buried her face in the petals. "Thank you for these," she murmured.

"I'll buy you a thousand roses, if they'll make you happy. I love you, Kamille."

"I love you, too. So much."

He scooped her up and carried her to the bedroom, kissing her over and over, whispering her name. She nestled against him, wondering how she could have doubted him—doubted *them*. They were meant to be together. And no one was going to stand in their way from now on: not the press, not the fans, not anyone.

PART II

THE NIGHT THAT CHANGED EVERYTHING

NINETEEN

KASS

Kass hurried down South Vermont Avenue, periodically glancing at her watch. The sidewalks were bustling with students and couples on Saturday-night dates. Crap! She was *so* late for her dinner with Eduardo.

As if he didn't have enough to be pissed about. The dinner had been her idea, so she could make it up to him for agreeing to go to San Diego with him last weekend and then canceling at the last minute. And in general playing hot and cold with him.

She wasn't sure why he hadn't told her to get lost, already. She hadn't exactly been the greatest . . . well, whatever she was to him. Part friend, part almost-girlfriend? Anyway, she'd done a lot of soul-searching lately and decided (finally) that Kamille had been right when they'd had their recent heart-to-heart. It was time for the chastity belt to come off—and for the emotional walls to come down.

Her cell buzzed. It was a text from Eduardo: WHERE R U?

5 MIN, she typed back. SORRY, TRAFFIC!

Which was a lie. She was running behind schedule because it had taken her half an hour to decide what to wear for the evening. Which was not like her. But she really wanted their date (yes, *date*) to be special, and it had taken her a long time to find something that made her look sexy and not so . . . *flat*. Why did Kamille and Kyle get all the boobs in the family?

Plus . . . she'd had important errands to run, like getting the bottle of champagne, which was chilling in the refrigerator with a Post-it note saying "HANDS OFF!" in case Kamille and Ballboy were tempted to help themselves. She'd also bought condoms at Rite Aid, just in case. She'd been so nervous and embarrassed bringing it up to the counter, mixed in with a bunch of other items she didn't even need, just to defuse the impact of the orange box with the words TROJAN ECSTASY spelled out so glaringly. The salesclerk had looked completely disinterested as he rang her up.

Kass turned the corner and spotted the restaurant across the street. As she headed for the crosswalk, she passed a newsstand.

Something caught her eye. It was the latest issue of *Dish* magazine, with a picture of Kamille and Chase on the cover looking tense and unhappy. The headline blared:

KAMILLE AND CHASE:
NOW WHO'S CHEATING ON WHOM?

"What the hell?" Kass said out loud.

She picked up the magazine. At the bottom of the cover was another, smaller picture, of Kamille hugging some guy.

Kass squinted. Was that Giles Sinclair? Her agent?

"Yeah, that's hilarious," Kass snorted, flipping through the pages. "These reporters are really scraping the bottom of the barrel." This was obviously a "follow-up" to the "story" that ran last week, with the picture of Chase allegedly hooking up with some girl at a club. Kamille had told Kass all about it, and how she and Chase had had a huge fight about it afterward, then made up with the "hottest sex" they'd ever had (like Kass needed that detail).

Kass wondered, not for the first time, if Kamille's relationship with Chase was entirely healthy.

"Are you paying for that?" the guy behind the counter snapped.

"What? Oh, sorry." Kass reached into her purse and handed him a five-dollar bill.

On page 28, Kass found the story about Kamille's alleged "torrid affair" with her "high-powered agent Giles Sinclair." There was another, perfectly innocent-looking photo of Kamille and Giles at some event. This was too much.

Then Kass's gaze fell on a bright red sidebar. She clamped her hand over her mouth to keep from screaming. It was a picture of her with the caption *Kamille's dumpy older sis—or is it her bro?*

In the picture, Kass was wearing her "ugly sweats," the ones she usually threw on if she had to run a quick errand and everything else happened to be in the wash. They made her look even more flat-chested than she already was, and were definitely not flattering. Her long hair was back in a ponytail, but the angle of the shot made it appear as though she had a mannish crew cut. Her face, devoid of makeup, was contorted, as though she were trying to suppress a burp.

Kass tried to think. She remembered wearing the sweats on Wednesday when she had to drop off some dry cleaning. Had some paparazzi followed her there and taken pictures of her? How *dare* they? And how dare they imply that she looked like a *guy*?

Fighting back her rage, she took a deep breath and read the paragraph next to the photo. It said that Kass was twenty-one, a junior at USC, a part-time employee at her mother's restaurant, and single. It went on to say that according to an "inside source," she was a closet lesbian in a hush-hush relationship with a fellow USC student named April Jansen.

"What . . . the . . . *fuck*?" Kass yelled. Even if she *were* a lesbian, closet or otherwise, she would never, ever hook up with that pompous little bitch April, who was in her small-business-management study group.

The guy behind the counter stared at her nervously. "Uh, you want your change? Magazine's only two ninety-five."

"No!"

Kass ran to the intersection, just barely catching the WALK sign, and crossed the street to the restaurant. Eduardo was waiting for her at one of the outside tables. His beer glass was almost empty.

"You made it." He stood up and kissed her on the cheek.

"You wouldn't *believe* what just happened!"

"What's wrong?"

She slapped the magazine on the table between them, practically knocking down the flickering votive candle and the tiny vase of pink sweetheart roses. *Oh, yeah.* She'd picked this restaurant because it was supposed to be romantic.

She stabbed her finger at the story about her. "*This!* I'm so *furious!* I think I'm gonna call a lawyer. Do you think I should call a lawyer?"

"Whoa, wait a sec. Sit down, Kass. Let me get you a drink."

"I don't *want* a drink, I want these people to burn in hell!"

"Kass. Please." Eduardo sat down and read the sidebar quickly. Kass sat down across from him, drumming her fingers on the table, waiting for his reaction.

"Yeah, this is pretty idiotic," he said after a moment. "But this is what tabloids do. I'd let it go if I were you."

"But how can they invade my privacy like that? I'm not the celebrity in the family! Kamille's the damned supermodel, with her famous baseball-player boyfriend and all that. It's one thing for them to write trash about her, about the two of them. But I'm just a regular citizen! And they *lied* about me!"

Eduardo reached across the table and squeezed her hand. "You're Kamille's sister, and that's enough. Look, I know this sucks. But don't let these media scumbags get you down. Let's just enjoy our evening, okay? I've missed you," he added softly.

"Enjoy our evening? How *can* I?"

Eduardo smiled patiently. "You said you had a big surprise for me. What is it?"

A big surprise? Right. This was the night Kass was going to

apologize to him for stringing him along. And take him back to her house and ply him with champagne and invite him into her bedroom, where that brand-new, bright orange box of Trojan Ecstasy condoms was waiting . . .

But she wasn't in the mood anymore. She felt so ugly and unsexy. And pissed off.

"Look." Kass yanked her hand away. "I'm sorry, but I can't. This . . . this *thing* has given me the mother of all migraines. Not to mention the fact that I want to *kill* someone right now. Can we reschedule?"

Eduardo frowned. "Kass. You keep 'rescheduling.' I'm beginning to think you don't really want to be with me."

"Excuse me?"

"Not that I was so sure to begin with. You're like the queen of mixed signals, you know that?"

"I'm really not in the mood to psychoanalyze our relationship right now, okay?" Kass said irritably.

"Fine."

"What does that mean, 'fine'?"

Eduardo stood up and put some money on the table. "I hope you figure out what you want, Kass," he said quietly.

With that, he was gone. Stunned, Kass stared after him as he headed down the sidewalk. "Eduardo! Wait!" she called out. But he didn't hear her. Or if he did, he was pretending not to.

Had he just broken up with her? Not that they were together, as he had (sort of) pointed out. But still . . .

Kass slumped back in her chair, trying to sort out her jumbled thoughts. This evening, which had started out so well and so full of promise, had taken a nosedive into hell. She was supposed to be having a romantic dinner with Eduardo. Instead, she was all alone at their table for two with nothing but a crumpled-up, hateful, lie-filled magazine. A magazine that had just ruined her life.

But she couldn't really blame the magazine, could she? Maybe she had overreacted . . . and then taken the whole thing out on poor Eduardo.

Kass buried her face in her hands and did something she never did.

She burst into tears.

TWENTY

KYLE

KYLE LAY ON THE COUCH, CLICKING THE REMOTE, wondering how there could be nothing interesting to watch—especially when they had about two thousand channels to choose from. A reality show about people who were addicted to reality shows? Seriously? And who the hell would watch something called *I Married My Brother: A True Story*? Talk about gross.

Oh, wait. *Double D-Lite* was beginning soon, which sounded fun. She had gotten into pornos about a year ago, partly because they were so hilariously fake, but mostly because her uptight mother absolutely forbade it. Fortunately, Kyle knew the password to get through the lame parental control feature. She would simply have to wait until Kat and Beau

were out the door. Which, judging by the sound of their conversation, was imminent.

> BEAU: Sweetheart, have you seen my belt with the
> fancy buckle? And what time's our reservation?
> KAT: Seven-thirty, honey. Movie's at nine-twenty.
> Did you check the top drawer of your dresser? Oh,
> by the way, did you remember to call your aunt
> Trudy about Thanksgiving dinner?

Kyle wondered if married couples always had such boring
conversations. She reminded herself to stay single, forever. She
continued surfing, coming across some random celebrity chef
cooking up a fancy pizza. Yum. She wondered if there was
anything decent to eat for dinner . . .

"Hi, doll!"

Kyle glanced up. Oh, God, it was her mother, dressed in a
red T-shirt, black silk shorts, and ballet flats. Apparently, she
was auditioning for the cast of *Glee*.

"Aren't you guys gone yet?" Kyle said, hoping she'd get the
hint.

"Just waiting for Beau. So! What are you doing?"

"I'm discovering a cure for cancer. What does it look like?"

"Very funny. Why don't you throw on an outfit and come
out with us?"

"No, thanks."

"We're going to Capriccio's for Italian."

Oooh, pizza. "Nah."

"You sure? We're seeing that new Steven Spielberg movie
after," Kat persisted.

"I have plans," Kyle lied.

"With who?"

"Like that's any of your business? Ash and Priscilla, if you must know."

"Okay. Well. You know where we are, if you change your mind."

Kat wandered off in search of Beau. Kyle turned her attention back to the TV screen. In truth, Ash and Priscilla were at a house party in Westwood tonight. Kyle was supposed to be there, too. But she'd blown it off, just like she'd blown off Graydon Garrison's party earlier.

The problem was, Ash and Priscilla were getting into increasingly hard-core stuff. Smoking pot was one thing, but coke and E? And what were those things called, whippits? A quiet night in with a porno and a bottle of tequila was more Kyle's speed. With Bree at a sleepover and Benjy out with his fellow drama nerds, she'd have the whole place to herself.

Kyle continued surfing channels. She wondered what was up with her mother's dinner invitation—and with all the invitations, lately. Last week, Kat had surprised her by picking her up after school to take her shopping. The day before yesterday, it was mani-pedis. The woman had obviously been reading self-help books or talking to a shrink about this. *Note to self: Bond with Kyle!*

Yeah, good luck with that, Mom, Kyle thought wryly. Although Kyle's nails, which were painted a shade called Toxic Taupe, *did* look sick. And she was never one to say no to free merch.

Half an hour (and a total waste-of-time discussion about which car to take) later, Kat and Beau were *finally* gone. Café

Romero was closed for minor renovations, so they were taking advantage and having a "date night," which was apparently what old people called going out. Kyle went to the kitchen to scrounge for dinner (a frozen pepperoni pizza—*yes!*) and retrieve the key to the liquor cabinet, which Beau kept quote-unquote "hidden" in a cracked Dodgers mug full of loose change.

Kyle heard the front door open just as she was settling back on the couch with her dinner, a bottle of Patrón, a Grand Canyon souvenir shot glass, and the opening credits of *Double D-Lite*. Crap! Had they forgotten something? She grabbed the Patrón and frantically tried to find a place to stash it.

"Hello?" A familiar voice came from the hallway.

It was Kass. What was *she* doing here?

"Kass? In here!" Kyle called out.

A moment later, Kass popped her head through the doorway. "Um, where is everybody?"

"Out."

"Oh."

Kyle stared at Kass, confused. Her sister's eyes were red, and her makeup was all streaky, as though she'd been crying. Which made zero sense. Like Kyle, Kass was not the crying type.

"What's up? You look like shit."

"Thanks. Hey, what are you doing with *that*? Do Mom and Beau know you're helping yourself to their liquor?"

Now *there* was the old Kass. "I'll get you a glass," Kyle offered.

"*No!*"

Kass ignored her and went to the kitchen. When she came

back (with a Niagara Falls souvenir shot glass—their father had been a collector), Kass was sitting on the couch, plucking a nonexistent dog hair from her not-entirely-ugly purple dress. (Fashion was not Kass's strong suit.)

"Cute outfit," Kyle complimented her. She poured two shots and handed one to Kass. "Tough day?"

"Yeah, you could say that." Kass took a sip. "*Wah!* It *burns!*"

"It's supposed to. And you're not supposed to drink it like it's a cup of tea, dummy. Watch and learn from the master." Kyle tipped her head back and downed her shot glass, demonstrating.

"Like this?" Kass followed suit.

"Like that! Exactly!"

"It's not too bad, if you like the taste of hydrochloric acid," Kass said sarcastically.

"Whatever." Kyle poured another round. "So. What's up? I wasn't kidding before when I said you look like shit."

This time, Kass finished off the tequila in one gulp. Then she picked up the bottle and helped herself to more. "My love life is a mess. I really, really screwed things up with Eduardo tonight."

"You have a boyfriend?" Kyle said, surprised. Dating was the other thing Kass never did, besides crying.

"No! He's not my boyfriend. Not exactly. He's in my econ class at school, and we hang out. The thing is, he wants more than friendship. And actually, I do, too, except that I've been kind of nervous about taking that next step because, well, he may *seem* like an amazing guy, but what if he turns out to be an asshole and just wants to use me for sex? Like Adam Kerrigan?"

"Adam who?"

"You don't remember Adam? My high school boyfriend? The love of my life?"

Oh, yeah, him. Kyle had a vague memory of a chemistry geek with bad skin and BO. Great boyfriend material. "So you and this . . . Edward, Eduardo haven't hooked up yet?" she said out loud.

"No. But tonight was going to be the night, maybe. I bought champagne and a box of—never mind, you're way too young."

"You bought *condoms*?" Kyle grinned. "So you were finally gonna get your V-card punched, huh?"

"My . . . what?"

"Your V-card? Or did you do it with that Adam guy? Never mind. Okay, so, what happened?"

"*Wellll* . . . we never made it back to my house, because we got into this awful fight."

"About what?"

"About this hideous picture *Dish* magazine published. Of *me*. And the stupid crap they printed."

"Really?" Kyle was totally confused. What could *Dish* possibly want with Kass? "Let me grab my laptop, I'll check it out."

"Don't bother, I brought it with me."

Kass reached into her purse and pulled out a rolled-up magazine. She unfurled it and turned to a dog-eared page, and handed it to Kyle.

Kyle took a look at the picture—and the story, too. God, no wonder Kass was losing her shit. If some pretend journalist had called *her* "Kamille's dumpy younger sis," then implied she looked like a guy, she would have been forced to kill the asshole.

"Yeah, this blows," she said after a moment. "You know, if Kamille wasn't such a fame whore, this wouldn't have happened," she added bitchily.

"Right? Finally, *someone* who agrees with me! *Thank* you!" Kass tipped back another drink.

"Yeah, her stupid so-called career is like a magnet for these media douche bags."

"*Exactly!* That's what I tried to tell—*whoa!* What are those people *doing*?"

Kass's eyes were suddenly glued to the TV screen. Kyle followed her gaze. A guy and two girls—or was that two guys and a girl?—were getting it on in a hot tub.

"It's the Nature Channel," Kyle joked. "I think this bottle's empty. You want me to grab another one?"

"Hmm? Yeah, sure. Ohmigod, what is he doing to her with his *tongue*?"

"I want to hear all about this Eduardo dude when I get back. Okay?"

"Hmm."

"And . . . Kass? When it comes to guys? You need to think less, hook up more."

Kass turned to Kyle and started giggling hysterically. "Think less, hook up more! Ha-ha, that's hilarious!"

Kyle raised her eyebrows. Kass giggling was about as rare as Kass crying. And dating. And, for that matter, getting drunk.

Kyle's night had suddenly gotten a lot more interesting.

TWENTY-ONE

KASS

KASS INSERTED THE KEY IN HER FRONT DOOR—OR SHE tried to, anyway. The key wasn't cooperating, and neither was her brain. Above her, the moon and the stars were swirling around, turning the night sky into a giant, blurry, cosmic video game.

She felt like throwing up.

The door opened abruptly. A fat middle-aged guy stood there, wearing nothing but a pair of boxers with tiny aliens all over them. Or were they martini glasses? He looked her up and down critically.

"I told them I wanted a blonde," he snapped. "With, uh, something on top. What are you, a Thirty-two-A?"

"What? Oh! I must have the wrong house!"

"This is two twenty-nine."

"I think I'm down the street somewhere. Sorry to bother you!"

Kass spun around and ran, or tried to run, down the sidewalk. She felt so dizzy, even dizzier than before, and what did that man mean, was she a 32-A? Was he talking about her address? A car drove by, honking, and then everything was quiet again. Except for the soundtrack to *Footloose*. Was she in a movie? Or was this a dream?

She finally reached her door. She checked first to make sure this was definitely her and Kamille's house. Yes, here was the terra-cotta frog. And the flowering cactus plants. And the blinking neon turkey hanging on the palm tree, in honor of Thanksgiving.

This time, Kass didn't bother with the key, which was way too complicated, almost as bad as calculus, and made her head spin. Instead, she rang the doorbell. "Kam? Are you home?" she shouted.

After a moment the door opened, and she found herself face-to-face with Kamille. Except that she was bigger and taller and blonder. And not Kamille. And not a girl.

It was Ballboy, wearing nothing but baby-blue pajama bottoms.

"Uh, hi?" Kass gave him a little wave.

"Hey. Did you lose your key or something?"

"Yes. Well, not really. Which way is my room?"

Chase laughed. Why was he laughing? "It's this way, party girl. You want a glass of water? And some Advil?"

"No, thanks, I'm really not hungry. Where's Kamille?"

"She's out. I was waiting for her."

Chase took Kass's arm and guided her into the front hall. She teetered a little on her heels, wondering why the ceiling and walls were shrinking and then expanding like the inside of a carnival fun house. She remembered, or thought she remembered, that Chase sometimes spent the night at the house. On occasion, she'd had to cover her ears to block out the noise of his and Kamille's arguments. Or lovemaking. Especially the lovemaking.

"Why are there diamonds all over the living room floor?" she said, suddenly noticing the bright, glittering jewels scattered across the carpet.

"What? Oh, that's broken glass. I gotta clean that up."

"Did Valentino break something?"

"Who?"

"Valentino. He's our dog."

"Come on, crazy, we need to get you into bed."

"Okeydoke."

And then the next thing she knew, she was lying down, and someone was pulling off her shoes. Chase. She closed her eyes, feeling his hands as they moved up to the waistband of her panty hose. How had she gotten from the front hall to this bed? Her bed? Maybe she and Chase had beamed over, like the people on *Star Trek*.

"Chase?" she murmured sleepily. "I should probably call you that, right? Since it's your name? I didn't mean to call you Ballboy behind your back. It's nothing personal. Well, maybe it is, because I wasn't sure I liked you, before. But you're actually kind of a nice person. Aren't you?"

"Yup."

Kass felt him turn her over slightly as he unzipped her

dress. "I'm so sorry about our fight earlier," she rambled on. "It's that stupid magazine's fault. I used to believe in the First Amendment, you know, freedom of the press and free speech and free love and . . . wait, where's Eduardo?"

"Who?"

"But now I think censorship's the way to go. Those magazines should be banned. Professor what's-her-name—the one with the big boobs, almost as big as those girls on Kyle's Nature Channel show—says that in Europe they don't put up with the kind of . . . hey, Eduardo? Did you get highlights? 'Cause your hair used to be black."

Silence. Kass felt strong, warm fingers massaging the back of her neck. "Mmm, that feels good," she murmured.

"Yeah?" Eduardo kissed her there, ever so gently.

"Mmm, do that again."

"Yes, ma'am."

His lips trailed deliciously down her back. Kass's entire body tingled with fire, and she arched herself against him. This was way, way better than . . . what had she been doing earlier in the evening? She couldn't recall. Yelling at someone and then watching a really excellent movie with Kyle? His arm encircled her waist, and he tugged tantalizingly at her panties.

Think less, hook up more.

"Take them off," she whispered.

"What?"

"Take them off."

Eduardo—it *was* Eduardo, wasn't it?—slid her panties down her legs. Her bra came off next. And then she was on her back, and he was on top of her, doing something to her breasts that made her gasp and moan and dig her fingers into his massive biceps. (Wow, had Eduardo been working out?)

"They're in the drawer, over there," Kass heard herself say.

"You sure?"

"Yes! I got them at Rite Aid today!"

"No, what I meant was . . . never mind."

He went away and returned a second—or was it a minute, or an hour?—later. Kass heard the lock on her bedroom door click shut. His breath reeked of whiskey, or maybe that was her. He mounted her, completely naked and unspeakably gorgeous, with those hard, rippling muscles and that tousled blond hair and those big blue eyes and . . .

She screamed. With pleasure. He was inside her, moving ever so slowly, then faster, then faster still.

She didn't remember Adam Kerrigan feeling this good. Not even close.

TWENTY-TWO

KYLE

"DIE, ASSHOLES!" KYLE YELLED.

She tapped the screen of Beau's iPad repeatedly, dispersing more grapefruit and strawberry bombs. They arced toward the killer zombies that were slowly stumbling their way toward her majestic princess castle. She had to kill the ones with the yellow eyes first, because they were the most powerful. The rest of them, the red-eyed ones, were useless—except when there was a pack of twenty or more, at which point their strength and speed increased exponentially.

Level three ended: 2,438 points. *Awesome.*

As Kyle waited for level four to start, she thought about Kass, wondering if she had made it home safely. Kass had taken off about an hour ago to make the ten-minute walk to the house she shared with Kamille. Kyle had tried to get her to crash in her old bedroom, but Kass had insisted on sleeping at her own place . . . "in case Eduardo comes over, plus I need to fold the laundry and do my taxes." *WTF?*

Kass had also insisted on driving, but Kyle had very cleverly taken her car keys away from her and hidden them in the refrigerator, in a tub of Greek yogurt. It was the smart thing to do, considering that Kass had personally polished off about a gallon of Patrón.

Level four booted up. Kyle sat up straight and adjusted the beach towel she was wearing. (It was a warm night for November, and she'd taken a spontaneous dip in the pool just after *Double D-Lite*.) One of the red-eyed zombies lurched menacingly across the drawbridge. Kyle repositioned her earphones, which were blasting the game's screeching metal sound track, and prepared to attack.

It was then that she felt a light tap on her shoulder.

She screamed and jumped to her feet. Benjy was standing behind her, smiling sheepishly.

"What the *fuck*?" Kyle shouted.

Benjy said something that she didn't hear. She realized that she still had on her earphones. She yanked them off and repeated: "What . . . the . . . *fuck*?"

"Sorry, I didn't mean to interrupt," Benjy apologized. "What are you playing?"

"Zombies versus Fruit Salad, if you must know," Kyle replied testily. "What are you doing here?"

"Um, I live here? I just got back from—"

Kyle fake-yawned. "That's fascinating. You can go now."

"Yeah, well . . . you might want to know that my dad texted

me before, and they're going to be home in like five minutes. And I'm not sure how psyched they're going to be when they see your party spread."

"What party spread?"

"This one?" Benjy waved at the coffee table, which was littered with two Patrón bottles, two shot glasses, pizza crusts, a bag of Double Stuf Oreos, and half a joint.

Oops.

"Yeah, I guess I'd better clean that up," Kyle agreed, massaging her temples. Her head was still spinny from the tequila, not to mention all the zombie-killing. "What time's it, anyway?"

A car door slammed outside. Benjy glanced around, then began methodically picking up the items and stashing them under the couch.

"What do you think you're doing?" Kyle demanded.

"Saving your ass."

"Huh?"

The front door opened. Coco and Chanel bounded down the stairs, barking. There was a peal of laughter—Kat's—then Beau's voice saying: "You think anyone's still up, darlin'?"

"That wasn't five minutes!" Kyle whispered furiously to Benjy.

In response, Benjy clamped his hand over her mouth and tackled her to the floor, behind the couch. Kyle tried to wriggle away, but he was too strong.

"Stop moving! *Shhh!*" Benjy hissed in her ear.

Footsteps, more laughter . . . then Kyle heard her mother and Beau walk into the living room and sink down onto the couch. They seemed to have no idea that she and Benjy were on the floor right behind them.

"That was fun," Kat said. "We should have a date night more often!"

"Date night's not over yet," Beau replied. "Mmm, come here."

"What are you doing, Beau? The kids!"

"I'm sure Benjy and Kyle're asleep by now. Mmm, you smell so good."

"Mmm, so do you."

Silence. Then kissy-smacky noises. Then heavy breathing. Then bodies shifting around on the couch. Then more heavy breathing. Then unzipping sounds.

"I want to see you naked."

"I want to see *you* naked."

Kyle's eyes widened in horror as various items of clothing came flying over the back of the couch: T-shirts, shorts, bra, panties, jeans, boxers, and more. Were the *parents* having *sex*? On the *couch*?

Ew!

"Oh my God, yes!" her mother moaned.

"You want more of that, baby?" Beau murmured.

Kyle turned her head to stare at Benjy. He looked as freaked out as she did.

Benjy put his finger to his lips and started belly-crawling across the floor, toward the dining room. He indicated for her to do the same; she obeyed.

Unfortunately, Coco and Chanel bounded over and began licking Kyle's face with their nasty dog-breath tongues. She wanted to tell them to cut it out, but she forced herself to keep quiet, for the sake of not getting grounded for the rest of her life.

After what seemed like hours, although it was probably more like minutes, Kyle reached the safety of the dining room. She got to her feet and followed Benjy, who quietly slid open the terrace door and stepped outside.

"Holy *shit!*" Kyle blurted out as soon as Benjy had closed the door. "Can you believe it? They were having *sex* right in front of us! That was like the most vomitatious experience I've ever had!"

"Yeah, we're probably going to be in therapy for like a hundred years," Benjy said. His gaze dropped. "Uh, Kyle? Speaking of naked . . ."

Kyle glanced down. She seemed to have misplaced her beach towel someplace between the living room couch and the terrace. All she had on was a pair of black boy briefs with the words GO FUCK YOURSELF on them.

"Ohmigod!" She crossed her arms over her chest. "Where . . . I mean, when . . . I mean, how long . . ."

"Just now. There's your towel, there, on the dining room floor. No worries, I didn't see anything."

"Bullshit!"

Benjy took off his Korn T-shirt and handed it to her. "Here, take this. I'm going to try to get upstairs somehow. I'm totally wiped. So, um, good night."

"Good night." Kyle slipped on his shirt, grateful for the coverage, even if it *was* Korn. "Hey, Benjy?"

"What?"

"You don't think I'm a slut, do you?"

Benjy started. "Where did *that* come from?"

"'Cause I'm not. I know I act like it sometimes. But it's just to confuse people, because I don't like everyone thinking they can figure me out." She added, "Besides, it drives Mom crazy."

"So . . . you're saying you *want* to drive your mom crazy?"

"Yeah. Sure."

"That is *such* a teenage cliché."

"Thanks."

Kyle wanted to say more, about that day they'd made out, about how fun and really nice it had been. How it *hadn't* been a teenage cliché. But she couldn't bring herself to do it.

"Hey, Benjy?"

"What?"

"Yeah, so I have this bio test coming up."

"Yeah?"

"It's gonna be a bitch."

"You want some help with it?"

"Sure! How about Monday after school?"

"Monday's drama club. How about Tuesday?"

"Tuesday's great."

Benjy waved and disappeared. Kyle stared after him.

And just like that, everything was okay between them again. Okay-*ish*, anyway.

TWENTY-THREE

KAMILLE

KAMILLE GLANCED AT HER WATCH: 1 A.M. TEN MIN-utes after the last time she'd checked.

"I'm gonna let him stew for a little while longer," she announced to Simone, who was on her third mojito.

"*What* are you guys fighting about, again?" Simone said, sounding bored.

"I told you, he got mad at me because I'm so crazed with work lately. We haven't had a lot of time together. But then he goes out with his buddies like once or twice a week, so what is he talking about, right?"

Simone raised her eyebrows. "That's all? I thought maybe he was cheating on you again."

Kamille glared at her friend. "Seriously, stop *saying* that! I've told you before, it's those awful magazines. They're constantly making up stories about him. About us. I hate them!"

Kamille picked up her mojito and finished it off, including the sprig of mint, which tasted bitter in her mouth. She tried to remember if she'd had dinner tonight. She hadn't. She and Chase had shared a pitcher of martinis at her place, then ordered in Chinese. But before they could sit down to eat, he had made a snide comment about her busy schedule, which had led to her snide comment about his "boys' nights," and the next thing she knew, they were yelling at each other. It had gotten so bad, she'd actually thrown the martini pitcher at him, which he'd dodged, and it had hit the wall and shattered into a million pieces.

And then she had stormed out. Outside the front door, she'd hesitated for a moment, to see if he might follow her like he sometimes did, begging for her forgiveness. He hadn't. So she had called Simone and told her to meet her at Skybar, ASAP.

Fuck him. Let him come crawling back, which he would surely do after enduring her absence for hours and hours. Frankly, if she had to, she could discipline herself to ignore him for days, even a week. She'd already been so good tonight, not returning his numerous texts and voice mails. Although they'd stopped around midnight, which had confused her. Maybe he'd fallen asleep? Or his phone had died?

"Excuse me. You're Kamille Romero, right?"

Kamille glanced up. A girl, probably around her age, was smiling and waving from the next table. She was with two identically cute guys.

"I love you!" the girl went on without waiting for a reply. "That ad you did? For that perfume? It rocks!"

"Thanks!" Kamille found herself smiling back. She wasn't used to getting compliments from fans. Or even *having* fans. It was kind of cool. "I have a new ad coming out, for Flower Power jeans," she volunteered.

"No fucking way." The girl stood up and turned around, pointing to the hot-pink rose embroidered on her back pocket. "Is that awesome or what?"

"Yeah, thanks for showing us your ass," Simone said under her breath.

"Simone!" Kamille hissed.

"I wouldn't mind seeing yours," one of the girl's cute friends called out to Simone.

Simone giggled. "Yeah? It'll cost you."

"Not a problem."

God, Simone was such a slut. But maybe she had it right. Maybe hooking up with randoms was better than having a boyfriend. Kamille seethed, thinking about Chase.

The cute guy bought Kamille and Simone a round of drinks. Then more people at the bar recognized Kamille and bought more rounds of drinks. At one point, some man in a fancy suit—the manager?—came over and whispered to Kamille that she could get a table and a comped bottle anytime she wanted, giving her his private contact info so she could bypass the formidable bouncers out front.

Many mojitos, and many autographs, and many cell-phone pictures later, Kamille was basking in the glow of celebrity adulation and in general feeling no pain. At one point, when some girl asked her about Chase, Kamille just burst out laughing and said, "Chase who?" Those words probably ended up being Tweeted all over cyberspace within seconds. But Kamille didn't give a shit. She was on top of the world (or on the rooftop of the Mondrian Hotel, anyway), surrounded by adoring fans she didn't even know she had, wearing a killer dress that she had actually been able to buy (versus rent) with her big, fat check from the Flower Power job. It was nice to have money after four years of struggling, wondering if she was ever going to be more than a waitress at her mother's restaurant.

Kamille wasn't sure, but after Skybar closed, the party moved to some club downtown. She had the vague, pleasantly surreal sense of being driven through the streets of the city in a limo filled with loud, drunk, happy people that maybe included Simone, maybe not. Had her friend gone home without her? Or checked into the Mondrian with the cute guy who joked about seeing her ass?

It didn't matter. What mattered was that she, Kamille, was on her way to becoming seriously famous. Like rock-star famous. She had fans now—real fans who wanted their pictures taken with her and who bought her expensive drinks. The owner (or whatever) of Skybar had treated her like a VIP. And at the moment she was even reveling in the fact that the paparazzi and the tabloids paid attention to her. So what if they spun lies about her and Chase? At least they were writing about her.

Chase. She closed her eyes wearily and wondered where he was, what he was doing. She wondered, too, when he would start appreciating her again, the way her (new) fans and friends appreciated her. A strange poison had seeped into their relationship lately. He used to love her so passionately, so unconditionally. The passion was still there, in spades. But the "unconditional" part . . . well, she wasn't so sure about that.

Was she not meant to be with him, after all?

Kamille's eyes flickered open. Maybe that was it. Maybe she was meant to be with someone else—someone nicer who didn't yell at her so much . . . who didn't make her want to throw martini pitchers at his head . . . who didn't get calls from people named Tiffani and Daria and Lise in the middle of the night. (Chase always had a legit-sounding excuse, but still.)

She reached for her velvet clutch and dug around for her cell. She checked to see if he had texted or called. He hadn't.

"Fuck. You," she said out loud.

"What?" A guy sitting across from her leaned over and put his hand on her knee, caressing it lightly. He was kind of hot, with curly dark brown hair and wide green eyes. Not Chase. Had he been at Skybar with the rest of the group? "You want to get out of here? I live close by, they could drop us off," he said with a wink.

"Sure," Kamille started to say. Why not? Maybe hooking up with this guy—whoever he was—would get Chase, get the poison, out of her system.

But instead, she picked up her cell again and composed a text. She typed: IM SORRY. I LUV U SO MUCH.

And then she hit send.

TWENTY-FOUR

KASS

K ASS SQUINTED AT THE BLINDING WHITE LIGHT THAT was burning up her retinas. When had her room gotten so . . . *bright*? And why did her head feel as though it was filled with thick, gooey cement?

She groaned and turned over. The clock on her nightstand blinked: 2:30. Two-thirty, as in the middle of the afternoon? Had she really slept that late? She always woke up at 7 A.M. sharp, alarm or no alarm.

There was only one explanation. She must be sick. She almost never got sick, as a result of her daily regimen of vitamins and herbal teas, plus her fastidious use of hand sanitizer. But obviously, these things had not been an adequate firewall. She knew that a bad flu was going around, and she *had* been feeling run-down lately. Finals week was coming up soon, and she had so much on her plate . . .

A loud, whirring noise came from somewhere in the house. Kass sat up abruptly—and immediately felt a wave of nausea unlike anything she had ever experienced before. She took a deep breath and tried to focus. What was that sound? Was there a burglar in the house?

The whirring noise stopped. Kass clutched her stomach and slithered out of bed, trying to be as silent as possible . . .

. . . whereupon her legs buckled out from under her, and she landed unceremoniously on the floor, ass first.

"Hey, doll! You up?" a voice called out.

Oh. Kass smiled, relieved, despite the fact that her body seemed to be falling apart. Not to mention naked. Where were her pajamas?

It wasn't a burglar; it was just Kamille.

Just Kamille.

KAMILLE!

It all came flooding back to her. Last night. The fight with Eduardo. The tequila-thon with Kyle. (*Damn* that little bitch!) Coming home. Running into Chase, alone.

And doing other things with Chase, alone.

Several times, in fact.

"I am so screwed," Kass muttered to herself. "I. Am. So. Screwed."

There was a knock, and the door opened, and Kamille walked in.

Kass braced herself for the barrage of swearwords. Or maybe the barrage of something else, like bullets.

"Hey, sleepyhead! Are you talking to yourself again?" Kamille said cheerfully.

"What?"

"I made mango smoothies, you want one?"

Kass blinked. Kamille was not coming after her with a gun or even yelling at her. She was offering her a mango smoothie.

In fact, she looked downright happy. Dressed in pink sweats and a matching tank top, and her face free of makeup, she was sunny, radiant. How did she manage to do this first thing in the morning? Oh, yeah, it wasn't first thing in the morning. And she was Kamille Romero. She was *always* beautiful, 24/7.

"Kam, I'm sick," Kass groaned, although she now realized that she wasn't sick from any flu. "My head, and my stomach . . ."

"Poor baby! Is that why you're all pasty white? And why you're sitting on the floor naked? Do you have a fever?" Kamille reached down to touch Kass's forehead with the back of her hand.

"Stop that!"

"I'm just trying to help; you don't need to be such a bitch about it!"

Kass winced. "Sorry, it's just that—"

"Just what?"

"I—"

Kass stared at the floor. What was she going to say? *I got really, really drunk last night and hooked up with your boyfriend! So sorry! It won't happen again! He's a sleazebag, anyway, and you're better off without him!*

Unfortunately, Chase wasn't the only sleazebag in this situation. Kass could only go so far, blaming her hideous lack of judgment on the tequila. If she confessed what she'd done to Kamille . . . well, Kamille would disown her. No question about it. In fact, the entire family would disown her. Kass would end up totally alone in the world, spending the rest of her life without the people she loved most.

She began to cry.

"Ohmigod, Kassie! Is it that bad? Where does it hurt? I'm calling 911!" Kamille insisted.

Kass shook her head. Which made it hurt even worse. "No, no, I'm fine. I was just, um, thinking about Valentino, that's all," she said, sniffling.

"What? Why?"

"I miss him."

"Doll, he's been gone for like seven years. But yeah, I miss him, too. Seriously, Kass, I think you should go back to bed. I can run out to the drugstore and get you some meds. I'm not meeting up with Chase till later, anyway. I can even cancel, if you need me."

"Wait, what? You're . . . meeting up with Chase?"

"Yeah. He and I had this humongous fight last night. In fact, I kinda broke our martini pitcher. Sorry. Not that you care about martinis, but still."

"You had a fight?"

"Yeah. I walked out on him and went out with Simone and these randoms till like three in the morning. I figured I'd ignore him and let him feel really, really bad about hurting me like that. Well, it worked, because when I finally texted him, he texted me back right away and told me how much he loved me and how he wanted to make it up to me. So I went over to his place, and we had like *the* most incredible sex, ever. Ohmigod."

Kass couldn't believe what she was hearing. "You . . . did?"

"Sorry, TMI, right?"

"But I thought he was *here*."

Kamille frowned. "He *was*. I mean, he was here in the beginning, when we had our fight. But he left after that, obviously, *duh,* because we met up at his apartment. Like four, four-thirty this morning. Kassie, why are you getting all OCD on me with these weird little details?"

Kass tried to think, which wasn't easy through the toxic haze of her hangover. When had she fallen asleep last night? Or, more likely, passed out? She tried to remember Chase getting dressed and leaving the house.

But all she could recall were the blurry images of his naked body pounding against her naked body . . .

"Sorry. Go on," she mumbled, trying to ignore the heat in her cheeks.

"With what? That's all. The point is, Chase and I are back together, and we're better than ever! He had this work thing he had to go to this afternoon. But he's taking me out tonight, to celebrate. I've gotta skip Sunday Night Dinner . . . you don't think Mommy and Beau'll mind, do you?"

"What? You *can't* miss Sunday Night Dinner!" Kass told her. *And you can't get back together with Chase,* she added silently. *He's a jerk. And I'm a jerk, too.*

"Just this once. It's really important to Chase. I'll tell Mommy I'm sick! You're sick, too, so she'll believe me! It can just be her, Beau, Kyle, Benjy, and Bree tonight—and whatever freaks she decides to invite."

"I don't think that's a good—"

"Oh, hey! Didn't you have a date with Eduardo last night?" Kamille interrupted. "How'd it go? Did you finally hook up, or are you waiting for a sign from God?" Her blue eyes sparkled merrily.

Kass turned away. "I think you're right, I need to rest. I'm gonna take a nap now," she mumbled.

"Oh! I'm sorry, sweetie! I'll leave you alone. Just call me if you need me, okay?" Kamille bent down and kissed her on the forehead. "Feel better! Love you, doll!"

"Love you, too."

Kamille breezed away. Crawling back into bed, Kass laid her head on the pillow and tried to think.

She *had* to tell Kamille.

But she *couldn't* tell Kamille.

What in the hell was she going to do?

PART III

CHRISTMAS

TWENTY-FIVE

KAMILLE

SIPPING A FLUTE OF VEUVE CLICQUOT CHAMPAGNE, Kamille gazed out at the gently sloping green and the sand-colored mountains beyond. It was a warm, dry December afternoon, perfect for a celebrity golf tournament in Palm Desert. Behind her, guests spilled out of the elegant Spanish-style clubhouse—more like a club *mansion*—and gathered on the stone terrace. Occasionally, the *thunk* of a golf ball or someone yelling "fore!" cut through the sounds of laughter and conversation and clinking glasses.

"Well? What do you think?" Simone came up to Kamille and tucked her arm through hers. "Do I know how to throw a sick party, or what?"

"Yeah, that's a nice way to describe an event to raise money for cancer awareness," Kamille said wryly. "Besides, you're just the assistant. Didn't your boss do all this?" She waved her hand at the elegant bistro tables, the tuxedo-clad servers, the outdoor raw bar, the jazz trio, the flowers, everything.

"*Just the assistant?* Bite your tongue, bitch! Don't you know that the assistant always does everything? No, you wouldn't know that, since you've never had a real job."

"Fuck you!"

"Mmm, girl fight. Can I watch? Or better yet, can I get between the two of you?"

Kamille smiled as Chase walked up to her and Simone, a wide grin on his face. He was dressed in pink-and-yellow plaid pants and a white polo that set off his deep tan—the tan he'd gotten during his and Kamille's recent getaway in Cabo, to celebrate his twenty-third birthday. He was carrying a club—no, *iron*—and swinging it lightly, as though practicing his driving—or was it *putting?* Kamille wasn't a golfer, but she'd tried to learn the terms, just to keep up with her boyfriend, who loved the sport almost as much as baseball.

"So how are you lovely ladies?" Chase said, draping his arms around Kamille and Simone's shoulders. Chase knew Simone from several double dates the four of them had been on (i.e., Chase, Kamille, Simone, and Simone's hookup du jour). Simone, unlike Kass and Kat, actually *liked* Chase and got along well with him.

"If you want a threesome, asshole, hire a hooker," Simone joked. "So how much money did you raise for us today? Forty thousand? Fifty?"

"Wrong. A *hundred*," Chase replied smugly. "Do I rock or what?"

"Wow, you definitely rock," Simone told him. "If Kamille wasn't here, I'd give you a blow job right this second."

"Really, Simone?" Kamille said, disgusted.

"Just kidding! Excuse me, guys, I've gotta go see if my favorite L.A. Raider needs something. Like a drink. Or an excuse to leave his wife. Poor guy, he looks so lonely!" She wriggled her eyebrows and drifted off in the direction of a tall, cute guy standing near the hors d'oeuvres table.

"She is so gross, I'm sorry," Kamille murmured to Chase. "Don't get me wrong, I love her like a sister. But still."

"Enough about Simone, let's talk about us," Chase said, pulling her in close and kissing her.

Kamille leaned into the kiss, sighing with pleasure. Things had been so good between them lately: no fights, no drama, no mystery phone calls from mystery skanks, nothing. Even the tabloids seemed to have eased up on them. And because the baseball season was over, he had tons of free time to just be with her.

Actually, Kamille was spending most of her nights at Chase's house in Holmby Hills lately. He'd told her right after Thanksgiving that he wanted to have her to himself, i.e., no roommate, i.e., no Kass. Which was fine with Kamille, since they no longer had to worry about privacy or being inhibited about making love on the living room rug, the kitchen counter, the dining room table, wherever . . .

Still, it meant that Kamille saw less of Kass than ever before. Plus, Kass was in the middle of final exams, so she was hardly ever at Café Romero these days. She'd even missed a couple of Sunday Night Dinners, to study, which was kind of unheard of. Kamille made a mental note to pin Kass down for a girls' night soon, just the two of them, to catch up. Kamille missed Kass, and she felt weird not knowing what was going on with her—like was she still going out with Eduardo? Did they ever hook up? Or had she found someone new through Lovematch? Basic, important stuff.

Chase's voice cut into her thoughts. "Hey, babe? Did I tell you, my mom invited us for Christmas dinner?"

"Yeah, about that." Kamille made a face and tugged at the front of his shirt. "I don't know what to do," she said quietly. "I've never missed Christmas dinner with my family, ever. But I don't want to disappoint your parents either. Especially not before I've even met them."

She and Chase had been trying to get down to Laguna Beach to see his parents for a while now. But between Kamille's shooting schedule—Giles had lined up two new ads for her, with Belladonna Cosmetics and some trendy new fashion designer with an unpronounceable name—and Mr. Goodall's numerous business trips (he was a lawyer for some big-deal firm), they hadn't been able to find a free day. She and Chase had spent Thanksgiving apart: he with his family in San Francisco, visiting with his elderly grandparents in their retirement home, and she in L.A. with her family. She'd hated not being with him for that holiday. She wanted to spend every holiday with him, now and forever.

"Do you think we might be able to see them for Christmas Eve instead?" Kamille said, pouting. "Or maybe go down the day after?"

"Um . . . not Christmas Eve."

"Why not?"

"Because I have special plans for us."

"You do? What kind of plans?"

"Sorry, I've been sworn to secrecy."

Kamille punched Chase in the arm playfully. "You jerk! Tell me!"

"Can't. This is, like, classified stuff. If I told you, I'd have to kill you." Chase plucked a glass of champagne from a passing server and gulped it down. "Anyway, how's this? Why don't we have Christmas dinner with your folks? I'll talk to my mom and see if she'd be okay with us coming down the day after. I'm sure she'll be cool about it."

"Really?"

"Really."

"That's a huge relief, thank you! You're the best!"

"Yeah, you can thank me later. At home."

"Mmm."

Chase kissed her again, more passionately this time. His lips tasted yummy, like champagne. As Kamille kissed him back, she was vaguely aware of a photographer nearby, taking their picture; she could hear the familiar, steady *click, click, click* of a professional camera.

But it was fine with her. She was getting more and more used to having her picture taken, and she didn't mind as long as the pictures were *nice* ones. Besides, Chase had mentioned just recently that his publicist, Zoe, wanted lots of PDA when they were out together, to reinforce their image as a super-happy, supertogether couple. If making out with Chase in public kept the media vultures from spinning lies about him, then Kamille was more than willing to oblige.

She felt Chase's hand sliding down her back, caressing softly. "Hey, are you wearing panties under that dress?" he whispered in her ear.

"Chase!" Kamille cried out, blushing furiously.

Chase hugged her, laughing. Kamille laughed, too. The photographer continued shooting: *click, click, click*. Feeling intoxicated from the champagne and the sunshine and the sheer, giddy joy of being with her amazing boyfriend, Kamille imagined the headline that would accompany these pictures on tomorrow's blogs: CHASE AND KAMILLE MORE IN LOVE THAN EVER!

This time, it would actually be the truth.

TWENTY-SIX

KASS

KASS WALKED—NO, SKIPPED—OUT OF THE FILM school building, clutching her backpack against her chest. She'd taken her last exam. The fall semester was over, done, finished. She could finally stop living in the library and start being a human being again.

She was not one to complain about hard work or a rigorous schedule. But this past "hell week" (and the weeks leading up to it) had been especially hellish since she'd overloaded on credits, which translated into more exams and papers than in previous semesters. She'd had enough caffeine, energy drinks, and not showering for a while. (She sniffed her armpit discreetly. Not too bad, thanks to Kamille's baby powder that she'd dumped all over herself this morning.) She wanted to take a long, hot bubble bath, drink a glass of wine (yes, wine!), and watch back-to-back episodes of *Buffy* on TiVo.

And tomorrow she planned to book a beauty day at the spa, using the about-to-expire gift certificate her mother had given her for Christmas last year.

And after that, she was going to call Eduardo. Finally. And apologize for freaking out on him over that stupid tabloid story about her being a flat-chested man or whatever. And see if he might give her another chance.

This was the new Kass. After her disastrous lapse in judgment right before Thanksgiving (she had nicknamed it the SHE, i.e., Stupidest Hookup Ever), she had gone through a brief period of depression, self-hatred, confusion. She'd consumed countless pints of Ben & Jerry's, lost sleep, and broken out in major zits trying to figure out what to do—all while juggling the pressures of studying for exams and writing several epic papers.

In the end, she'd decided not to tell Kamille what happened between her and Chase. She wanted to put the SHE monster behind her. What good would it do to break Kamille's heart—not to mention sever their sisterhood and best friendship forever? And possibly get strangled in the process? (Kamille was definitely the most temperamental one in the family.)

So Kamille and Chase were still together. Big deal. Their relationship wasn't long for the world, anyway. Kamille had never lasted more than a few months with any of her boyfriends. Besides, once a cheater, always a cheater, and Chase was sure to dump Kamille for someone else any day now. Or else Kamille would catch him in the act, one or the other. Kass intended to remove herself from their drama-filled, dysfunctional equation and move on. She had her own life to live.

Thankfully, Kamille hadn't been around much, which had made it easier for Kass to cultivate her Noh mask, her fake smile, her neutral-friendly voice. ("How are you and Chase doing? Good? I'm so *happy* for you!") Kamille was busy with her modeling, and she was crashing at Chase's house most nights. And Chase seemed to be avoiding any contact with Kass. In fact, she hadn't seen him at all since . . . well, since the SHE. Which was fine with her.

The thing was, Kass actually felt *good* now. Hopeful. Light—as though a weight had been lifted off her shoulders. And strangely, miraculously, she was eager to jump-start the spark she'd had with Eduardo. As awful as it sounded (and she would never admit this to anyone, least of all Kamille), her terrible tryst with Chase had made her realize that she actually *liked* sex. Wrong person, yes, but all the right feelings, sensations, impulses. She was eager to experience them again, this time with the *right* person.

With Eduardo, if he would have her?

Kass continued down the path, breathing in the cool, crisp air, grinning to herself. Loud rock music was blasting from a dorm window, and someone let out a euphoric scream. Students celebrating the end of the semester. She had to stop by the business school to pick up a paper. Then she had a date with Buffy . . .

She spotted him walking out of Marshall. She hadn't expected to run into him. Not today. Not with dark circles under her eyes and her armpits reeking of baby powder. Had thinking about him made him materialize like this? Was some mischievous Cupid god messing with her?

"Hey." Eduardo stopped in his tracks and adjusted the

backpack on his shoulder. His face was as much of a Noh mask as hers was around Kamille.

"Hey." Kass pushed back a lock of (greasy) hair and gave him a little wave. "How are you? I haven't seen you in ages."

"Yeah, not since the econ exam on Monday? How'd you do?"

Well, of course, she'd seen him in econ. Sitting two rows over and not looking in her direction, not once. That wasn't what she meant.

"I think I did okay? Although that essay question about globalization kind of tripped me up."

"Yeah, me, too. I think Professor Mueller threw in a super-hard one just to be nasty."

"He's such a sadist. I'm so glad that class is over. I won't miss him at all."

"Yeah, me neither."

Silence. They stepped aside to let a girl pass with her rolling suitcase dragging behind her. A couple of guys walked by, talking animatedly about their digital photography final. In the distance, somebody yelled, "Fight on!," and then more voices joined in. The USC battle cry. Kass stared at the ground, wondering if she should say something, or just wish Eduardo a happy holiday and take off. She really should at least wash her hair before she tried to win Eduardo back . . .

"Listen. Eduardo." Her voice cracked.

Eduardo gazed at her. At that moment she saw something in his eyes . . . something familiar, warm, wistful. Not Noh-like at all.

It was all the encouragement she needed. To hell with a makeover. She dropped her backpack to the ground, threw her arms around his neck, and kissed him.

He hesitated only for a second, then kissed her back. Kass melted into his embrace, his lips, giving in to the moment completely. It was better than the empty physical heat she'd shared with Chase . . . *way* better, because she cared about Eduardo. A *lot*.

"Get a room!" someone called out.

Kass stepped back, breathless.

"Um . . . wow!" Eduardo said, laughing awkwardly. "Does this mean . . . are you . . . that is, are we . . ."

"Yes," Kass said, nodding happily. "I am. We are. This is my apology—for being such a jerk."

"Um . . ." Eduardo laughed again. "Look, I'd love to pursue this further, and I guess we have a lot to talk about? But I have to race home and pack. I'm flying home tonight, to Austin, to spend Christmas with my family."

"Oh!"

"Maybe I can call you?" he suggested.

"Yes, definitely! Please call me!"

Eduardo smiled and touched her face. "You're nuts, you know that, right?"

"Yeah, I know."

"It's a good thing I like crazy girls, then," he joked.

Kass grinned.

He turned and left, waving. Kass stood there watching him go, positively goofy with happiness. Everything was right with the world again. It felt like Christmas morning, and it wasn't even the middle of December yet.

TWENTY-SEVEN

KAT

CRADLING A GLASS OF 1982 CHÂTEAU MARGAUX IN her hand, Kat regarded the carnage of presents, gift boxes, wrapping paper, and ribbons under the tree. It looked as though a storm had passed through their living room.

Christmas. It was her favorite day of the year, mess and all.

She wandered over to the dining room and gave the dinner table a last look. She and the girls had set everything out earlier, including the red embroidered tablecloth and napkins that David's grandparents had brought over from Hungary . . . the napkin ring holders that her mother had made out of antique silver spoons . . . and the nice china, the white-and-gold Wedgwood, which had been her and David's wedding pattern.

She knew she had so much to be grateful for. Beau. Her incredible children. The restaurant. She remembered those terrible days after David had died, not knowing if she was going to be able to survive, to raise the girls on her own, to pay the bills. But somehow, she had created a new life for them all. It wasn't perfect, but it was good. Some days, it was even great.

And on this day, it seemed downright amazing. The delicious smell of roast turkey wafted from the kitchen. Her favorite Christmas CD, by Ella Fitzgerald and Louis Armstrong, was playing on the iPod dock. The Château Margaux was sublime, from David's personal collection of "special-occasion wine."

Unfortunately, she was down to the last three bottles of it. She wondered what it would be like when she opened the very last one.

She felt the sharp sting of tears in her eyes. She raised her glass in the air and whispered, "Merry Christmas, sweetie, wherever you are."

"*Mommmmmy!* Coco threw up on my *shoooooooes!*"

Bree ran into the dining room, looking so pretty and way older than her ten years in her formfitting red velvet dress and red lipstick. Bree had taken to calling Kat "Mommy" lately, which pleased her to no end. (Their real mother, Angie, who was spending the holidays in the French Alps with a twenty-one-year-old ski instructor, apparently insisted that her children call her by her first name.)

Kat turned away slightly so that Bree wouldn't see her crying. "Where did you get that lipstick, young lady?" she demanded.

"Ky let me borrow hers. Mommy, my *shoes!* They're *gross!*"

Kat took a peek. Bree was holding a pair of black wedges

that were most definitely "gross," covered with something resembling guacamole. Coco had probably been eating crayons again.

"Set them down, honey. I'll get some paper towels," Kat said with a sigh.

At that moment Benjy and Kyle ambled into the dining room arm in arm. Benjy was so handsome and grown-up looking in a navy-blue suit, white button-down, and gray tie (which Kat recognized as one of Beau's). Kyle was more casual (if that was the right term?) in a black vintage tux, Sex Pistols T-shirt, and purple high-top sneakers. Kat started to tell her to go change; dressing up for the holiday dinner was a die-hard Romero (now Romero-LeBlanc) family tradition. She herself was in an emerald-green Dior that she wore only for the holidays.

But she willed herself to keep quiet. It was Christmas, after all, and she didn't want to get into an argument. Besides, Kyle *was* dressed up, in her own weird, unique, Kyle sort of way. She'd even bothered to style her short auburn hair in curls and put on glittery makeup.

"When's dinner?" Kyle said, grabbing an olive off the crudités plate.

"Soon. Kamille and Chase should be here any second. And your dad—I mean Beau—is getting changed. Where's Kass?"

"She's upstairs taking a nap," Bree piped up. "Mommy, my *shoes*!"

A nap? In the middle of the day? Maybe the Christmas-morning excitement had been too much for her.

Tending to Bree's shoes, Kat thought about Kass, about *all* her children. They were doing so well these days—no major crises or drama. Thank God. Kass was done with her semester, and she seemed much more cheerful lately, and much less stressed. Kat had overheard her talking on the phone with someone last week—an Eduardo?—and her voice had sounded so animated, so happy. Maybe a new boyfriend was responsible for her good mood?

As for Kamille . . . her modeling career was thriving. She was still dating Chase, whom Kat continued to have doubts about, although their relationship seemed to have waned in the media spotlight, which was progress. Kat secretly wished Kamille would break up with him and find someone less . . . *controversial.* But that would come in time. Kamille was young, and Kat predicted many, many boyfriends in her future.

As for the other kids . . . well, Kyle's GPA was up to a 3.2, and Kat had gotten only a couple of calls from the school administration recently (versus the usual two, three times a week). Benjy and Bree were such good kids and so responsible and never caused Kat or Beau a moment of trouble. She wondered, not for the first time, how they had turned out so remarkably well with the globe-trotting, booze-swilling, man-eating Angie as their mother—correction, *one* of their mothers. What had Beau ever seen in her? She was certifiable. Of course, she also looked like Sofia Vergara.

Beau came downstairs just as Kat was finishing up cleaning the green dog vomit. He was wearing his traditional Christmas outfit: black tuxedo pants, black smoking jacket, and a red silk tie with a picture of Santa Claus on it.

"Hey, sweetheart," he called out. "Smells incredible. Everyone here?"

"We're just waiting on Kamille and Chase."

"Wow, you look hot. Am I allowed to say in front of the kids—hot?"

Kat blushed. "Yes, you're allowed."

"*Ew,* you guys," Kyle complained. She, Benjy, and Bree wandered into the living room and started hip-hop dancing to "Rudolph the Red-Nosed Reindeer."

Kat went over to Beau and wrapped her arms around his neck. "Hey."

"Hey."

"Do you love me?" she whispered, suddenly feeling vulnerable.

Beau hugged her fiercely. "I'm crazy in love with you, you know that," he whispered back.

"And you married that other woman, why?"

"Because you were already taken. 'Sides, I could ask you the same question. About David. But I won't."

Kat pulled away and stared into Beau's eyes, which had become dark, inscrutable. This was a subject they never discussed.

Although maybe, one of these days, they should open one of David's special-occasion bottles of wine and do just that?

"I love *you,*" Beau went on solemnly. "The day we got married was the happiest day of my life, right there next to when Benjamin and Brianna were born."

"Really?"

"Really. Darlin', what is it about Christmas Day that makes you feel so . . . fragile? Is that the word I'm looking for?"

That was *exactly* the word. Kat smiled slightly, marveling at how her husband always knew her better than she knew herself.

"I just love you so much, and I love our children so much," she said passionately. "I just want us all to be happy and healthy and safe and . . . well, you know."

"I know."

"I only wish that—"

But she was interrupted by the sound of the front door opening. Kamille pranced in, hanging on Chase's arm. Kamille had on her faux-mink jacket over a long, slinky black gown and pearls. Chase, in a dark gray suit and tie, was *GQ*-gorgeous, as always. They both looked a little drunk.

"Guess what?" Kamille cried out. "Guess what guess what guess what?"

"What, doll?" Kat pulled away from Beau to greet Kamille and Chase.

Beaming, Kamille held out her left hand and wriggled her fingers. On the ring finger was a ring.

A diamond ring.

An *enormous* diamond ring.

For a moment Kat couldn't breathe. Or speak.

And then she found her voice. "Oh . . . my . . . *God!*" she burst out. "Kamille, I don't understand. How can you even think about—"

"Can I be a bridesmaid? Can I be a bridesmaid?" Bree cut in excitedly.

Kyle sauntered over and kissed Kamille on the cheek. "Congratulations or whatever. Just promise me you're not gonna wear one of those puffy white princess dresses, 'kay?"

"Yeah, 'cause you're the fashion expert in this house?" Benjy joked. "Congratulations, you guys!" he said to Kamille and Chase.

Chase grinned. "Thanks, man."

Beau enfolded the two of them in a massive hug. "Wow! I am speechless! And that's not something that happens to me often. Kat, honey, let's break open some champagne! The expensive stuff. I think we should have the wedding in Dodger Stadium, don't you? Just kidding, I promise I won't be one of those parents who take over the wedding planning . . ."

"You're getting *married*?"

Kat turned around. Kass was standing at the bottom of the stairs, pale as a ghost.

"Kass, you're up," Kat said, forcing a smile. "Dinner's ready. How was your nap?"

But Kass didn't reply. She was staring at Kamille with an expression Kat couldn't even begin to translate. Shock? Anger? Confusion? In response, Kamille was giving Kass an incredulous "what the hell?" look. And Chase—well, Chase had dropped his gaze to the ground as though his black Prada loafers had suddenly become very, very interesting.

What was going on?

"Oooo-kay, so who's gonna help me get the champagne?" Beau said loudly. He, too, seemed to sense the weird tension in the room.

"Me me me!" Bree said, jumping up and down.

"All right, pumpkin, as long as you promise not to drink it all."

"Ha-ha, Daddy!"

Still in shock over Kamille's news, and now doubly worried about Kass's strange reaction, Kat just stood there frozen as Beau and Bree went to get the champagne . . . and Kyle and

Benjy went to change the music . . . and Kamille and Chase went to help themselves to the Château Margaux. (Couldn't they wait for the champagne?)

Which left just her and Kass in the front hall.

"Doll, you okay?" Kat asked her gently.

Kass wouldn't look at her. "I'm fine. I, um, need to go upstairs and, um, make an important call. I'll be down in a sec, okay?"

"Kass, what's wrong?"

"Nothing. Just start without me."

"But—"

Kass didn't wait for the rest of Kat's sentence. She turned around and raced back up the stairs. A moment later, Kat heard a door slam shut.

And now Kat was alone.

So much for a drama-free Christmas.

TWENTY-EIGHT

KASS

KASS LAY DOWN ON HER OLD BED, TUGGING THE QUILT up to her chin, still reeling from Kamille's news. She could hear the strains of "Jingle Bells" coming from downstairs, and laughter, and the unmistakable *pop!* of a champagne cork.

What an *awful* Christmas.

Kass used to love this holiday, especially when her father was alive. When she, Kamille, and Kyle were little, he even dressed up as Santa Claus and pretended to come down the chimney. He and Kat would go crazy with the presents, the decorations, the food, everything.

Kat tried to keep some of the old family traditions going, like the funny notes from "Santa" in each of their stockings and the rice pudding with a single almond in it, on Christmas Eve. Whoever got the almond was supposed to be the next one to marry. (Last night, Bree was the winner, so the system was obviously flawed.)

But somehow, it just wasn't the same without her father. No offense to Beau. But he was no David Romero.

And David Romero would have never allowed the likes of Chase Goodall to marry his daughter, much less date her. He had been so smart about people, with what he used to call his "bullshit radar." He wouldn't have fallen for Chase's smarmy, all-American, nice-guy act the way Beau had. It was so painful, watching Chase sucking up to Beau and pretending to be interested in his ancient baseball stories.

Kass sighed.

She glanced around her old bedroom, which she hardly ever used anymore. It was very similar to her *old*-old bedroom back in their other house (the one she thought of as their "real" house); her mother had made sure to paint the walls of this one the identical shade of peachy apricot and arrange her belongings in exactly the same way. There were the trophies from her debate tournaments and ice-skating competitions. There was her National Honor Society plaque.

And there was her old dollhouse. She and Kamille used to play with it for hours: feeding their dolls, bathing them, putting them to bed. There was a nasty dent in one corner of the roof, from when Kamille had gotten mad at Kass about some stupid thing or the other and kicked it down the stairs. She and Kamille had fought about that for days . . .

Kass's gaze shifted to her desk, to the souvenir snow globe

from their family trip to New York City, and the photo-booth pictures of her and Kamille from high school, and the maroon USC mug filled neatly with pens and pencils.

Next to all that was the slender white box she'd bought at Rite Aid yesterday, when she'd realized that her period was late.

"Stop stalling," she told herself, and got up from bed.

She knew that she was probably overreacting. Even though she was as regular as clockwork, period-wise, it was possible to be off because of stress and other factors. The last month or so had been sheer insanity, with exams and papers and catching up on holiday shopping (which she usually finished well before December—but not this year).

And, of course, the SHE.

But Kass needed to be sure. Now more than ever, since Kamille had decided to go and get herself engaged to her sleazy, two-faced BF.

Making sure there was no one in the hall, Kass took the box and tiptoed quietly to the bathroom next door, which she used to share with Kamille. Benjy seemed to have taken it over; there was a can of shaving cream and a razor on the sink, and tiny beard hairs all over the place. Plus a pair of rumpled black boxers on the floor. *Ew.* She locked the door, went over to the toilet, and sat down.

Kass pulled the instructions out of the box and read the tiny print once, twice, three times. She wanted to make sure to do this right. Pee on the stick? How was she supposed to pee on something so small? But, whatever. She pulled down her panties and positioned the stick. And started to pee. And stopped to inspect the stick. And started to pee again, stick in place. Was she doing this right?

Afterward, she did as the instructions said and placed the stick on a flat surface—i.e., the sink—using a clean tissue to keep it from being contaminated by Benjy's disgusting little beard hairs. She checked her watch and started timing. Five minutes. Okay. While she waited she read the instructions once more, in English *and* in Spanish. She learned all about HCG, human chorionic gonadotropin, the hormone the test was supposed to measure in her urine. If she had a certain amount of it, the test would come out positive. Two thin blue lines. If she didn't, it would be negative. One thin blue line.

"Kassie! *Dinnerrrrrrrrr!*" She could hear Bree shouting up the stairs.

"I'll be right there!" Kass shouted back.

She glanced at her watch. Thirty seconds to go. Then twenty. Then ten . . .

Taking a deep breath, she looked at the white pee stick lying on the counter.

Two blues lines.

No.

There had to be a mistake. Kass picked up the stick and held it up to the light, shifting the angle this way and that.

There they were. Two solid, unmistakable blue lines.

"Kassie!!!!!"

Kass began shaking all over.

PART IV

JUNE GLOOM

TWENTY-NINE

KAMILLE

KAMILLE STUDIED HER REFLECTION IN THE MIRROR, AT the way the shimmery ivory fabric clung to her figure in a sexy-but-not-slutty way.

"I looooove this dress!" she squealed. "It's a Vera Wang. What do you think, Kassie?"

No response. Kass was sitting on a chair flipping through a bridal magazine. Actually, it wasn't even a bridal magazine. It looked like a workbook from school.

"Kass? Kassidy Marie Romero? *Hellooooo?* Um, Kass? It would be nice if you could join us today," he added irritably.

"What?" Kass glanced up from her workbook and adjusted her glasses. She had started wearing them a couple of months ago, and they made her look even more egghead-y than she already did. "Oh. Sorry. Spanish homework. Yeah, that dress is fine, Kam."

"That's what you've said about *all* the dresses I've tried on today," Kamille pointed out. "Kassie, you're my maid of honor. I really need you to step up here."

"Sure. No problem."

Kamille ran a hand over the ruffly bodice, making sure the tiny microphone was still securely taped to her boobs, and turned her attention back to the mirror. Being filmed was her new "normal" ever since Hank and his crew had started following her (and her family and Chase) around Los Angeles and documenting the wedding preparations.

She still had mixed feelings about selling the TV rights to her and Chase's wedding to the Life Network, which was producing a reality series called *Happily Ever After*. When Giles had pitched the idea to her back in January, she'd said no at first. But the money was good—no, *great*—and Chase had really been into the idea. So she'd finally agreed, and she'd gotten the rest of the family on board, too.

The rest of the family except for Kass. Sure, Kass had *technically* signed on. She had *said* she was willing to go along with the shoots, which took up a lot of time and energy and were a new and bizarre kind of intrusion into all their lives. Kamille still wasn't used to having cameras present during meetings with her wedding planner (the fabulous Courtney Powell) . . . heart-to-heart talks with her mother about the ups and downs of marriage . . . and dates with Chase. Especially the dates with Chase. Kamille felt so self-conscious arguing or making out or whatever in front of the cameras, knowing that a TV audience would be seeing the footage in just a few months.

But. Kass was Kamille's maid of honor. Not to mention her best friend in the entire world, and, of course, her big sister. So why couldn't she make more of an effort? If Kamille could get over her camera shyness, so could Kass.

Instead, Kass had been acting like a zombie ever since production began . . . frankly, ever since Christmas, when Kamille and Chase announced their engagement. Kass was supposed to be superhappy and supportive, all giggly and girlie and throwing Kamille lingerie showers and such. Instead, she was basically sleepwalking through her role as maid of honor, on and off camera. And it was already April. The wedding was only two months away! Kamille needed Kass more than ever now, since Chase was so busy with the start of the baseball season.

Could Kass get over her Inner Envy Bitch or whatever and be there for Kamille, already?

Hank gave a signal. "And . . . we're rolling!"

Kamille beamed at the mirror. "This is my favorite dress so far. What about you, Kassie?"

But Kass was scribbling away in her Spanish notebook, oblivious.

"Stop, stop, *stop!*" Hank rubbed his eyes. "Why don't we take a break? Meet back here in fifteen? We'll go grab some coffee, and . . . Kamille? Can you talk to your sister, please?"

"Um, sure."

As soon as Hank and the crew had left, Kamille sat down next to Kass, being careful not to wrinkle the dress, which cost more than all the dresses in her closet at home put together. She took a deep breath, trying to channel "calm" and "patient," which were not exactly natural to her.

"Kass, what's going on?" she said, calmly and patiently. "You're totally not into this. The wedding, I mean. And every time I try to talk to you about it, you just get all weird and quiet."

Kass said nothing.

"Kassie! *Talk* to me!" Kamille's voice grew more shrill. So much for calm and patient. "I can't *stand* this anymore! What is wrong with you, anyway?"

Kass lifted her head. "You can't marry Chase," she stated simply.

"*What?*"

"You can't marry Chase. He's no good for you."

Kamille balled up her fists. Was her sister out of her mind? How *dare* she? "What kind of horrible, bitchy thing is that to say?" she shouted. "You're just jealous because Chase and I are madly in love and you don't have a boyfriend! That Eduardo guy dumped you because you're totally uptight about sex! You need to see a shrink! You need to—"

"I'm pregnant," Kass blurted out.

Kamille started. "W-what did you say?"

"I'm pregnant. I'm five months along."

Kamille's gaze dropped to Kass's stomach. She couldn't make out a baby bump. On the other hand, she *had* noticed that Kass was into even baggier-than-usual clothes recently.

"Oh . . . my . . . God!" she gasped. She reached over and hugged Kass, then immediately backed off. "Ohmigod, I'm sorry! Did I hurt the baby? Ohmigod, congratulations! Why didn't you say anything before? Are you happy? Is Eduardo happy? I'm such an idiot, I thought you guys had broken up, but obviously I was—"

"He and I aren't together. And he's not the father," Kass interrupted.

"He's not? Then who is?"

Kass shook her head. "Never mind."

Kamille stared at her sister. Her head was reeling. This explained so much about Kass's behavior lately. It was the pregnancy hormones. Kamille had heard that they were way, way worse than the usual period ones.

"Does Mommy know?" Kamille asked her. "And the rest of the family?"

"Nope. Not yet. You're the first."

"Wow, really?"

"Really."

Kamille smiled and hugged Kass again, more gently this time. "Sweetie, I'm *so* glad you told me. And I'm totally going to be there for you! I'll be your labor coach. Can I be your labor coach? And I'll go to Lamar classes with you!"

"You mean Lamaze?"

"Yeah, Lamaze! And we can go shopping for baby stuff together! There's that supercute baby store next to the Starbucks in our neighborhood. You'll need a crib and a high chair and a stroller and lots and lots of baby clothes. And all those random little things, too, like bibs and sippy cups, and what did Kyle used to call them when she was a baby? Kikis and nanas and babas."

As Kamille babbled on, she was vaguely aware that Kass didn't seem all that psyched about Lamaze classes or baby clothes or kikis or nanas or babas. But that was okay. Kamille understood now why her sister seemed so out of it. Single motherhood, raging hormones, getting fat . . . it couldn't be easy.

Kass had always been there for her, the perfect big sister (except these past few months . . . but she had a good excuse). Now it was time for Kamille to take care of Kass. She would see her through this pregnancy, even help her raise the baby as much as she could. Of course, Kamille would have a new husband and *their* children to think about soon enough. But for the moment Kass would be her priority. Kass and her beautiful new baby. Kamille's niece or nephew.

Unless . . . the father planned to be in the picture? But Kamille didn't think this was the right time to ask. She would wait for a better opportunity, when Kass wasn't acting quite so *moody*.

THIRTY

KASS

"YOU'RE PREGNANT?" KAT GASPED. "AS IN, BABIES-pregnant?"

"Yeah, that's what *pregnant* usually means, Mom," Kass replied. "I'm keeping it. It's due in August. And that's about all I'm going to say on this subject."

She peered at her watch. "We should get to work. The rest of the staff's going to start arriving any minute now, and we're booked solid through ten o'clock."

Silence. Kat and Beau stared at her with stunned, deer-caught-in-the-headlights eyes. Kyle pulled out her phone and started texting—probably to Benjy (who along with Bree was spending a rare weekend with their mother, Angie, at her

Brentwood house). Kamille squeezed Kass's hand under the table and smiled encouragingly.

Kass wondered why no one was saying anything. And why did she have to pee again? Did all pregnant women spend their entire days peeing? She shifted uncomfortably in her chair and glanced around the dining room, trying not to feel like a complete freak. She could hear Fernando prepping back in the kitchen; other than him, they were the only ones there, at least for the next few minutes when more employees started arriving.

Kass had picked this setting to break the news to the family, for precisely that reason. It limited their ability—specifically, her mother's ability—to have a nervous breakdown and/or ask a million personal questions that Kass had no interest in answering.

Beau was the first to break the silence. "Well, you know we're all one hundred and ten percent here for you, honey," he said awkwardly. "Money, TLC, help with the baby, a place to live . . . whatever you need, sweetheart."

"Thanks."

"I think it's totally cool," Kyle said, continuing to text. "I didn't think you had it in you, Kass. You're like the family slut now!"

"Kyle, that's quite *enough*!" Kat snapped. "Kassidy, who is the father? Is he going to take responsibility?"

Oh, God. Kass wondered how many times she was going to be asked about Annabella's dad. Annabella Grace Romero. She'd had a vivid dream last night that the baby was a girl, and that she had named her after Grandma Romero and Grandma Ferguson.

"That topic is way off-limits," she stated firmly. "Anyway, I have a plan. I talked to my adviser, and we figured out that I can take the fall semester off and still have enough credits to graduate with my class next June. Of course, I'll have to hire someone to take care of the baby spring semester onward. I've already signed up for this website that has a database of qualified nannies."

"Oh, really?" Kat folded her hands on the table, which meant that she was about to give a lecture. (Kass and her sisters knew that gesture well.) "I'm not sure if you've thought through the economics of having a child on your own," she went on primly. "How do you plan to finance this nanny? We pay you a good hourly wage here, but you only work part-time, and that's not enough to cover child-care costs. And what about health insurance premiums? And grocery bills? Are you planning to breast-feed or bottle-feed? Do you even know what formula costs these days? And don't even get me started on the price of disposable diapers, especially the so-called environmentally responsible ones—"

"Mom, I've already thought through all these things. And more," Kass cut in. She adjusted her glasses, which she'd had to wear these last few months because the pregnancy hormones were wreaking havoc with her vision and she couldn't see as well with her contacts. "I know this isn't going to be easy. It will probably be the hardest thing I've ever done. But this baby is coming in four months, and she—I mean, she *or* he—is my responsibility. Yes, I'll have to make sacrifices. But I will make it work." She added softly: "I have to."

But her mother wasn't finished. "Have you been seeing Dr. Chen regularly?" she rambled on. "Are you taking prenatal vitamins? Have you had an ultrasound yet? Are you getting enough calcium and protein in your diet? And folic acid? What about pregnancy yoga classes? They offer those at the gym, you know? And what about—"

"Yes, yes, yes, yes, yes, and yes. Was that enough yeses? Mom, please don't worry, I've got this under control."

Kat sniffed. A tear rolled down her cheek. "How can you say that? You're going to have a baby! Ohmigod, I'm going to be a grandma!" she exclaimed.

"Sweetheart, it's okay," Beau said, putting his arm around her shoulders. "Kass sounds like she knows what she's doing. She always does."

Yeah, well, not exactly, Kass thought. Her sexual awakening aside, the SHE had been her lowest moment, ever. And now she would pay for it for the rest of her life.

She *had* considered terminating the pregnancy. It was just after Christmas, when she realized that *not* terminating would mean the end of her education, her career, and her ties to the family. To Kamille, especially. She kept picturing Kamille's face—*all* their faces—when she announced that she was pregnant with Chase's baby. The image of it made her want to curl up and die.

But she couldn't go through with an abortion either. She just couldn't. It was an impossible dilemma. She stayed in bed through New Year's, telling everyone she was sick. The fog of despair and indecision had actually lasted for several weeks. Kamille kept asking her what was wrong, and Kat, too; she told them both it was a lingering bad cold.

Then, slowly, gradually, she came out of the darkness. She decided to keep the baby. She formulated a course of action: how to juggle her classes, her job, and being a single parent.

This was what she did best: organizing, strategizing, making lists. The start of the new semester and being back at school helped to sharpen and focus her mind.

Her *other* big decision had been to not tell Kamille (or anyone else) about the baby's paternity. She would keep Chase's identity a secret. Of course, it meant that Kamille would marry him not knowing what a complete and total scumbag he was. But if that was the price to pay for Kamille and the family not hating Kass forever and ever . . . well, then, so be it.

And then there was Eduardo. Who had called . . . and called and called. She hadn't returned any of his messages for a while, and then finally gotten her act together long enough to e-mail him and say that she had met someone else over the Christmas break. It was a cruel, horrible lie, and sure to make him never, ever speak to her again. But she didn't know how else to break things off with him. She cared about him so much, but there was no way she could be with him when she was pregnant with Chase's baby.

As for Chase . . . thankfully, he had stopped coming by her and Kamille's house altogether. He had even stopped coming to the Sunday Night Dinners. It was easy enough for him to avoid the dinners, especially once spring training began and he was on the road so much. And miraculously, Kamille didn't seem to suspect that anything was wrong.

Except for one tiny detail. The stupid reality show. Why had Kamille and Chase agreed to air their wedding (and all the preparations leading up to it) on national TV? Everyone was expecting Kass to be a chipper, gung ho cheerleader of a maid of honor for those millions of future viewers. Instead, it was all Kass could do not to throw up whenever Kamille wanted to discuss wedding details with her on-camera (should it be a daytime or evening ceremony? . . . should they write their own vows or rip off something from the Internet?), or talk honeymoon (St. Lucia or Paris? . . . hotel or private condo? . . . should they squeeze in a quick getaway between games or postpone until the end of the season?).

Kass sighed. She would just have to do better. She had become quite the actress lately in her real life. Why not do it for the TV cameras?

KASS INSERTED HER KEY IN THE LOCK, PUSHED THE DOOR open, and stumbled into the front hallway. She was so tired from work that she could barely stand. The fatigue was the toughest part physically, besides the cravings (salmon for breakfast—WTF?—and chocolate anything 24/7) and the constant trips to the bathroom. Not to mention the mood swings and the headaches and the weight gain and the vision thing and the itchy belly (why?). How did other women do this? At least the morning sickness had stopped, sometime after Valentine's Day. (The irony of vomiting on that particular holiday hadn't escaped her.)

The family meeting earlier had gone well. Sort of. They had all behaved pretty much as she'd expected, and Kamille had been happily clueless. It was all Kass could ask for.

Just then, she felt a strange movement in her stomach.

"What was *that*?" she said out loud. Had she eaten something bad? Maybe the salmon and chocolate binges were catching up to her? Was she sick? Or, God forbid, was she going into premature labor?

She reached under her shirt and touched the curve of her belly gingerly. It happened again: a soft, almost imperceptible fluttering, like butterfly wings grazing her insides.

Kass gasped. And giggled. Ohmigod, the baby must be kicking!

"Hey."

Kass screamed. Chase was standing in the doorway to the living room, smiling sheepishly.

"Sorry, didn't mean to scare you," he apologized.

Kass took several deep breaths, trying to still the mad racing of her heart.

"You okay?" Chase asked her.

"What in the *hell* are you doing here?"

"I let myself in with my key."

"Kamille gave you a key?"

"Ages ago. Look, I wanted to talk to you. I figured this was the only way. Kamille's waiting for me back at my house. She thinks I'm having a beer with my manager."

"Yeah, lying to her is like second nature to you, isn't it?" Kass scoffed.

"I could say the same thing about you."

Kass glared at him. "What do you want?"

"Kamille told me. About the baby. Is it mine?"

Kass knew this conversation had to happen sooner or later. She took another deep breath and told herself to just repeat the lines she'd rehearsed, over and over.

"No, it's not yours," she said calmly. "The dates don't add up."

"She said you're five months pregnant. We . . . that . . . was five months ago."

"So what?"

"So you're a liar."

"And you're an idiot. The father's a guy I dated. We did a DNA test, and it's a hundred percent match. I won't tell you his name, because he's not in my life anymore, and he's not going to be in the baby's life either," Kass fibbed.

Chase looked startled. "You did a DNA test?"

"Yeah. We did a DNA test. So please get out of my house. Now. I'm tired, and I need to get to bed." Kass added, "And please leave me your key. Kamille shouldn't have given it to you without asking me."

"You haven't said anything to her, have you? About—"

"No. And I never will. And neither will you."

"Believe me, I won't."

"Good!"

"Yeah, whatever."

They stared at each other for a moment, like two opponents on either side of a line in the sand. Kass had forgotten how insanely good-looking he was, But she didn't feel anything in response, like attraction or lust or longing. She only felt anger and regret.

And, of course, anxiety. Could Chase tell that she was lying through her teeth? Was the memory of that fateful night buried in his subconscious beneath all those booze-soaked brain cells? Someday, somehow, would he recall that he had been too drunk, or horny, or lazy, or all of the above to open that brand-new box of Trojan Ecstasy condoms? Or would he even demand a DNA test of his own?

Then what would he do?

THIRTY-ONE

KAT

"DO YOU THINK KASSIDY'S GOING TO BE OKAY?" KAT asked Beau worriedly.

"Hmm?" Beau was lying in bed next to her, reading the morning paper. "She's going through some tough times, but she's the strongest girl I know, next to you," he reassured her.

"I hope you're right."

Kat was still adjusting to Kass's news, a month after her big announcement. She remembered when she herself found out that she was pregnant for the first time, with Kass. Unexpectedly pregnant. It was hard enough, going through all that when she was just twenty-three. At least she'd had David. Kass was doing it all on her own.

"What about Kamille? Do you think *she's* okay? I mean, is she *happy*?" Kat went on.

"Of course she's happy, darlin'. Why do you ask?"

"I don't know. It's all happening so fast. Her modeling, her engagement, this reality-TV show . . ."

"That's Kamille for you. If she doesn't have drama and excitement going on every second of her day, she's bored to death. You know that." He picked up the sports page and flipped through it.

Kat studied her nails; she was way overdue for a manicure. She knew deep down that Beau was right. And yet . . . she couldn't shake the feeling that Kamille was on autopilot, racing through her crazy daily schedule without stopping to think things through or to even take a breath. She no longer came into the restaurant because she was just too busy. And when she was there, the camera crew was always with her. Like the other night when Kamille and Kass were speculating about Chase's bachelor party while they sampled the specials in the kitchen. Or last week when the cameras caught all three girls arguing about Kamille's choice of bridesmaids.

The phone rang. For a moment she thought it might be Kass, inviting Kat to come along to her ob-gyn appointment today, after all. (Weren't mothers *supposed* to do that? Why did Kass insist on going to all these doctor visits alone?)

But it was the landline, not the cell. Kass never called on the landline. Almost no one did.

Kat reached for the phone on her nightstand. She didn't recognize the number on the caller ID. She really *did* need a manicure, desperately. Pippa had told her that one of the many downsides of hitting menopause was excessive chipping and cracking. *Great.*

"Hello?"

"Kat Romero, please."

Her chest tightened at the sound of the official-sounding voice. "This is she."

"Mrs. Romero, this is Lieutenant Sanchez from the Irvine Police Department."

Oh dear God in heaven. Kat knew, just knew, that something bad had happened to one of her children. This was the same call she had gotten almost five years ago, when she got the news about David's accident.

But . . . Irvine? So many miles away? That didn't make any sense.

"Mrs. Romero, are you still there?"

"I'm here."

"Sweetheart, who is that?" Beau whispered.

Kat put her finger to her lips. "Lieutenant Sanchez, what is this call in regard to?"

Beau raised his eyebrows. "Police?"

"I wanted to let you know that one of my men came upon a wallet belonging to your husband," Lieutenant Sanchez explained.

Kat started. She turned to Beau. "You didn't tell me you lost your wallet," she said in a low voice.

"What are you talking about, honey? It's right here."

Beau pointed to the nightstand on his side of the bed. His wallet was sitting next to his "World's Best Dad" coffee mug from Bree, his laptop, and his big, messy pile of loose change and receipts.

"My husband has his wallet. He just checked. You must have made a mistake," Kat said to the lieutenant.

"I'm sorry, I didn't make myself clear. I meant your *late* husband. Mr. David Romero."

Kat's gasped. "W-what did you say?"

"One of my officers found it in an abandoned home yesterday. It looked like it had been there for some time. It contained a bunch of credit cards, his driver's license, his Social Security card, a few other pieces of ID, and two hundred dollars in cash. Oh, and a whole lot of family photos."

Kat closed her eyes. She knew exactly which baby, school, and wedding photos Lieutenant Sanchez was talking about. She could still picture them, after all these years, just the way David had arranged them. "I don't understand. What does this mean?" she said out loud.

"I can't answer that question, Mrs. Romero. I'm assuming he didn't take the wallet with him when he went sailing that day? In any case, I wanted to let you know, and also to make arrangements to get the wallet to you . . ."

But Kat was barely listening. Her thoughts were racing with this bizarre new development. David's wallet had resurfaced after all this time . . . in *Irvine* of all places. How did it get there?

She remembered that day—that terrible, terrible day—when she'd gotten the news about his accident. He had gone sailing in the waters off Marina del Rey alone, saying he needed to clear his head about something. He didn't usually sail solo, and she would have questioned him more about it as he was leaving the house. Except that the phone was ringing, and FedEx was at the door, and Kyle was late for her ortho-dontist's appointment, and Kamille had spilled juice on her favorite dress, and Kass's hard drive had crashed in the middle of some important homework assignment . . .

When the storm came up, he had called her on his cell and said he was heading back in. That was the last she ever heard from him. His boat, called *The Kassidy,* had turned up the next day, broken and battered, on a rocky, isolated stretch of beach near Malibu. His body was never found.

And now the police had come upon his wallet nearly five years later? In Irvine? She couldn't even begin to wrap her brain around this. David used to keep all his belongings in a waterproof sack when he went sailing. Was it possible that the sack had turned up on shore, separately from the boat, and that some random person had picked it up? But if that was the case, why didn't that person turn it in to the police before? Or take the cash?

When she finally hung up, Beau leaned over and cradled her face in his hands. "What's happening, sweetheart? What's this about David's wallet?" he said quietly.

"I'll tell you later," Kat replied in a trembling voice. "Can you just hold me? For like an hour?"

"I'll hold you all day if you want."

Kat nestled in Beau's arms, feeling numb. She lay like this for a long time. She knew she should just get up and get started with her day—she wanted to go to the gym, and she had a doctor's appointment at eleven, and there was so much to do at the restaurant—but she couldn't seem to move.

She had spent all these years putting her life back together: healing, rebuilding, moving on. And just like that, with a single phone call, she had plummeted back to the past. A past that (if she had to be completely honest) she had never quite made her peace with.

THIRTY-TWO

KAMILLE

"OHMIGOSH, OVEN MITTS! THANK YOU, GRANDMA Ferguson!"

Kamille fake-smiled and did her best to sound polite. Enthusiastic, even. She didn't care so much about Grandma Ferguson or the rest of the bridal shower guests; she mostly cared about the TV cameras that were trained on her. She didn't want to come across to her future viewers as some sort of spoiled bitch who only wanted Tiffany and Bloomingdale's.

Even though that's exactly what she wanted.

Grandma Ferguson beamed. "You're welcome, dear! I knitted them myself for you and Charles."

"*Chase.*"

"What, dear?"

"Chase!"

"What are we chasing, honeybunch?"

Kamille sighed. "Nothing, Grandma."

She turned the hideous puke-tan oven mitts over in her hand, wondering how much longer the shower was going to last. She gazed out at the dining room full of relatives (close, distant, and unidentifiable) and friends (ditto), all of whom had agreed to sign release forms and wear microphones so they could be filmed for the show. Four TV camera guys were positioned in different strategic spots, missing nothing, and the lighting crew had transformed Café Romero from a cozy restaurant into a brightly lit set.

Kat was going from table to table greeting their guests and also overseeing the food and drinks. Kamille wasn't sure, but her mother seemed preoccupied about something.

Looking bored (as usual), Kyle thrust another present at Kamille, wrapped in silver paper with the word FOREVER on it in fancy cursive. All the girls in the bridal party had been assigned a job, and Kyle's was to hand Kamille her gifts.

"I think it's wineglasses or whatever," Kyle said in a low voice. "I can hear broken glass inside." She put the box up to her ear and shook it.

Kamille heard it, too. "Oh, fuck!" she said loudly, before she could stop herself. Hank, the director, gave her a withering look. She was definitely not supposed to drop the F-bomb when they were filming. She mouthed "Sorry!" and began unwrapping.

Kass was sitting in a chair nearby, balancing a legal pad on her lap and jotting down which gift was from whom. That was *her* job, so Kamille could write everyone thank-you notes later. Kamille couldn't imagine having to write a hundred thank-you notes by hand—hadn't anyone ever heard of group e-mails? But Hank wanted to make a scene out of it. He'd even suggested that it might be "funny" if Kamille and her sisters mixed up the envelopes and sent the wrong thank-you notes to the wrong people. *Yeah, LOL!*

Kass was tired looking and cranky, as usual. Some women seemed to blossom with their pregnancies; Kass was the opposite. The show's makeup crew had done their best to cover up her dark circles and splotchy skin. (Did being pregnant give a person zits? Kamille was going to have to be careful with that one when she and Chase started their family.) They'd also tried to get her into a nice, stylish maternity outfit, versus the oversize black T-shirt and baggy leggings that had become her daily uniform, and contact lenses (like she used to wear) instead of her nerdy glasses.

But Kass wasn't having any of that. She could be so stubborn—almost as stubborn as Kamille. And Kyle. And Kat. It must be a Romero family trait.

After the (broken) wine goblets came the next present, in a large gift bag with a picture of Winnie-the-Pooh on it. A pair of white leather baby shoes hung from the massive pink-and-pastel-blue bow.

Winnie-the-Pooh? Baby shoes? Kamille was confused. She reached inside and pulled out something that looked like a small gaming console.

"It's a breast pump for when you can't be there to nurse your little one," her great-aunt Beatrice spoke up from one of the center tables. "They didn't have those when I was young! You put it on your breast, like this, and when you flip the switch your milk comes out." She demonstrated with her hands.

"Yeah, Kamille. I bet Chase'll love helping you with that," Simone called out, giggling.

Really? In front of Aunt Beatrice and all the other old ladies in the room? And Chase's *mom,* for God's sake? "Shut the fuck up, Simone," Kamille snapped.

Hank gave her another scathing look.

"I meant, shut the *heck* up. Aunt Beatrice, you're so generous! And thoughtful! But you know, *Kass* is the one who's having a baby. I'm getting married. This is my wedding shower."

"Oh!" Aunt Beatrice frowned. "Which one is Kass? Is he the tall boy with the glasses?"

Kass slunk down in her chair.

Just get this thing over with, Kamille told herself. Chase was waiting for her at home with a bottle of her favorite Chardonnay on ice. They were going to have a rare night in, together, without the cameras. She couldn't wait.

Kyle handed Kamille more gifts. As she opened them, she cast a sideways glance at the large table of Goodall women in front: Chase's mother; Chase's sister, Amanda; a couple of aunts; and an assortment of cute blond cousins ranging in age from eight to eighteen. Chase's mom didn't look like she was having a good time. In fact, she was staring pointedly at her skinny diamond watch, like she had somewhere very important she'd rather be.

Kamille had finally met Mrs. Goodall and Amanda and the rest of the family the day after Christmas, when she and Chase had driven to Laguna Beach to announce their engagement. She was surprised to find that somehow, they weren't the superhappy, supertight clan Chase had made them out to be. His father was a big drinker. His mother didn't drink at all but quoted the Bible a lot. Amanda seemed weirdly possessive about Chase and kept making snide, bitchy comments to Kamille. Chase's two brothers sat in front of the TV the whole time watching football and ignored everyone.

Chase had apologized about them afterward, saying that it had been an "off" night and they hadn't been themselves. Kamille wasn't sure what to think; he hadn't taken her back to Laguna since that time, and today was the first time she'd seen any of the Goodalls since then.

But really, who cared? Kamille was marrying Chase, not Chase's family. And he was practically perfect. Especially in the last five months since their engagement. Sure, he was busy with the team and on the road so much. But when he was home, he was so sweet and attentive to her. For a brief period, around New Year's, the bad fights and the binge-drinking and the drama had resurfaced again. But then they went away again. These days, their relationship was stronger than ever.

"Last one," Kyle whispered as she gave Kamille a large pink box.

Kamille opened it. It was her gift from Chase's mom: a leather-bound Bible. With rainbow-colored Post-it notes sticking out of it.

"Oh, wow, thank you so much!" Kamille said through clenched teeth. *Smile and be polite,* she reminded herself. She had nothing against Bibles—in fact, quite the opposite. Still, it seemed like a weird wedding shower gift, especially with the Post-it notes.

Mrs. Goodall patted her platinum-blond updo. "I've marked the important passages for you. The ones about how to be a good wife to my firstborn son."

Kamille stared at her with wide eyes. *Wow.* Mrs. Goodall was just about the craziest woman she'd ever met, which was saying a lot. And she was about to become Kamille's mother-in-law.

Maybe she and Chase *should* start drinking heavily again.

THIRTY-THREE

KYLE

"SHALL I HEAR MORE? OR SHALL I SPEAK AT THIS?"
Benjy said in a stage whisper.

"'Tis but thy name that is my enemy," said the pink-haired girl beside him. "Thou art thyself, though not a Montague. What's Montague? It is nor hand, nor foot, nor arm, nor face, nor any other part belonging to a man. O, be some other name! What's in a name? That which we call a rose by any other name would smell as sweet . . ."

Kyle leaned back in the auditorium seat, put her feet up, and watched Benjy in action. He and the pink-haired girl were rehearsing a scene from *Romeo and Juliet* by Shakespeare, for the Wesley Eastman Academy Drama Club.

She had to admit, it wasn't awful. It was actually really *not-*

awful. She'd read Shakespeare plays for school, and his dusty, archaic words had put her to sleep faster than cough syrup and Grand Marnier shots (her personal remedy for insomnia). But spoken out loud and acted onstage, they were kind of interesting. And smart. And weirdly psychological.

Her phone buzzed. It was a text from Bree, who was home alone.

HIIIII KY! ☺))))

Seriously? Again? Bree had taken to texting her a lot lately. Today seemed to be a record, with twenty, maybe thirty texts. For some reason, Bree seemed to harbor the bizarre idea that she and Kyle were BFFs. Still, Kyle knew Bree was at the house by herself, waiting for her and Benjy to come home. The parents were off running some mystery errand in OC.

Kyle typed:

HEY BRIE CHEESE. EVERYTHING OK?
YESSSSSS!!!!! R U COMING HOME SOON LOL? ☺))))
YES. MAKE U DINNER K?
K LUV U LOL!!!!!! ☺))))

Kyle tucked her phone back in her pocket and turned her attention back to Benjy and the pink-haired girl, who were wrapping up their scene. Mr. Weaver, the drama teacher, wandered out from the wings, waving a dog-eared script in his hands.

"Fabulous! Super!" Mr. Weaver gushed. "But, India, if I may? It might be nice to see a little more of that youthful, let us even say immature *je ne sais quoi* from you. Remember, our Juliet's only thirteen." He clapped. "All right, then, why don't we rewind and run quickly through Romeo and Benvolio, Act One, Scene One? Is our Benvolio here?"

"He's out sick," the pink-haired girl, India, said. "I'm taking off now, I've gotta go study for my SATs."

Benjy glanced around the stage. "Hey, Javier, can you be Benvolio today?"

"No, man, I'm trying to keep this effing prop from falling down," Javier replied, holding up a roll of duct tape. "Can't you get someone else to do it?"

"Yeah, like who? Everyone left." Benjy steepled his hands over his eyes and peered out at the audience. "Kyle, is that you? Hey, can you come up here and read some lines with me?"

Kyle sat up. "Dude, I'm just here to give you a ride home."

"Come on. A favor. It'll take like five minutes."

Kyle rolled her eyes. "Fine. Whatever. Five minutes, okay?"

"Great, thanks!"

Kyle walked up to the stage, hoping that her slumped posture and scowling face were communicating her displeasure to Benjy loud and clear. She did not like being pressured into doing . . . well, *anything*.

When she reached Benjy, she thrust out her hand. "Okay, *what* am I reading?" she snapped.

Benjy handed her a script and pointed to a highlighted section. "There. You're Benvolio. I'm Romeo. We're cousins."

"Is Benvolio a girl?"

"No, a guy."

"No way. I've gotta play a *guy*?"

Benjy grinned. "That's why they call it acting, Kyle."

Kyle sighed. "Fine. God! Let's just get this over with."

"Five minutes, I promise."

Kyle glanced at the highlighted words on the script. "Tell me in sadness who that is . . . I mean, who *is that* you love," she read out loud. The words felt awkward on her tongue, all twisted and convoluted. "What the fuck? What does that even mean?" she asked Benjy.

"Romeo is in a funk because he thinks he's in love, and Benvolio's trying to get him to talk about it," Benjy explained. "Come on, pretend you're bullshitting Kass or Kamille into spilling their secrets. You're good at that, right?"

"Ha-ha." Kyle turned her attention back to the script. "Tell me in sadness who is that you love," she repeated, more slowly and earnestly. Okay, *this* time she'd nailed it.

"What, shall I groan and tell thee?" Benjy said.

"Groan! Why, no. But sadly tell me who."

"Bid a sick man in sadness make his will. Ah, word ill urg'd to one that is so ill! In sadness, cousin, I do love a woman."

"I aim'd so near when I suppos'd you love'd," Kyle said lightly.

Aim'd so near. Ha-ha, that was clever! Like Shakespeare was comparing Benvolio's mental guessing games to shooting an arrow at a target. Kyle was beginning to like this play. Or at least, not hate it.

The five minutes passed quickly, and she actually found herself enjoying the process of reading through lines. Even though subbing as Romeo's boy cousin for the high school drama club wasn't exactly a glamorous Hollywood gig. She'd always imagined her acting debut on an HBO miniseries, or maybe a cool indie movie that would premiere at Sundance, so she could walk the red carpet wearing something completely inappropriate and flip off the reporters. Still, this experience didn't completely suck.

"Hey, you totally impressed Mr. Weaver," Benjy told Kyle on the car ride home. "He gave me a flyer to give to you. It's for this production he's directing over at the community center this summer. He thought you should audition for it."

Kyle's mouth curled up in a half smile. Cool. So the old drama teacher thought she was good?

"Yeah, well, I'm really, really busy this summer," she said out loud. She wasn't about to let Benjy know that she might be interested in trying out for this play, whatever it was. She probably couldn't get a part, anyway. She didn't have acting experience, like that India girl. "Besides, you were supposed to be ready to be picked up like an hour ago," she bitched. "My mom made me come get you because she and your dad had to go to Irvine."

"What's happening in Irvine?"

"The fuck should I know? Anyway, we have to go straight home and heat up dinner for you, me, and the Bree. I swear, she was texting me like constantly this afternoon. She needs a hobby, like maybe a new puppy to take care of."

"You know this, right? She had to write an essay for school last week about her 'personal hero.' She wrote about you."

"She did *what*? Why?"

"Ask her to show it to you. It was like, 'My big sister Kyle is the smartest person I know, blah, blah, blah.'"

"Shut the fuck up."

"I'm serious."

Kyle stopped at a red light behind an idling yellow Ferrari. The traffic this time of day was insane. She drummed her fingers on the steering wheel, thinking about Bree's crazy essay. And smiled. So maybe it wasn't the worst thing in the world, having *one* person in the family who appreciated her.

She glanced over at Benjy. Or *two* people in the family. He *had* been kind of not-lame to her this academic year, helping her with her homework and encouraging her to get into acting and so forth. And in general keeping things sane in the midst of all the insanity: Kamille's over-the-top fame-whore wedding, Kass's soap-opera pregnancy, being trapped in the living room while the parents were having gross old-people sex, etc., etc.

"What?" Benjy grinned. "Why're you staring at me?"

The light turned green. Kyle slammed her foot on the accelerator and sped up, relishing the look of fear on the Ferrari driver's face as she passed him. "I was thinking that your haircut makes you look like a girl," she told Benjy. "A really ugly girl."

"Gee, thanks."

"You're welcome. Come on, let's get home and microwave some shit."

Kyle was in a good mood all of a sudden. Which usually didn't happen to her unless she was on something. Hmm, maybe she *didn't* need pot and tequila and all that crap to make her life not completely suck? Which was a revelation.

THIRTY-FOUR

KASS

"OKAY, LADIES, LET'S SQUAT DOWN AND PRACTICE OUR Kegels!" Candy, the overly cheerful Lamaze instructor, chirped at the class. "Coaches, let's help our partners get into position!"

Kass grabbed onto Kyle's arm so she could lower herself into a squat without falling flat on her (massive) butt. God, this was humiliating. She was six, almost seven months along, and she was absolutely *huge*—not like one of those skinny pregnant women who pranced around with tiny, almost imperceptible baby bumps until their babies were born. She felt like a farm animal, enormous and lumbering. It probably didn't help that she'd been hitting the Double Stuf Oreos and chocolate-chip ice cream in a big way lately.

She swore to herself that she would take up Pilates (and weight lifting and marathon running) as soon as Annabella was born. The day after, even. She could be the most disciplined, determined person in the world when she put her mind to it. Unfortunately, her mind was in a supersized, slow-motion, Oreo-and-ice-cream haze these days.

"Hey, Kass? Why is Candy Bar making you do Kegels?" Kyle piped up. This was her first ten minutes at her first Lamaze class ever, and she had already given the instructor a nickname. Normally, this would amuse (or annoy) Kass. Today, it just made her hungry. "Is that so you can have superhot pregnancy sex?" Kyle rambled on.

"Um, no? It's so we have strong muscles for pushing out our babies," Kass replied testily.

"Good. 'Cause I can't imagine any of you getting it on with those ginormous bellies. You'd crush the other person to death, if you know what I mean."

"That's a really nice thing to say. Thanks a lot."

"Or would they just stay on top the whole time? Wow, this is fascinating! Yeah, maybe I'll check and see if there are any pregnant-lady pornos out there . . ."

Kass sighed. She wasn't sure what was worse, having Kamille or Kyle as her labor coach. Kyle definitely beat Kamille hands down in the "deranged" category. Kamille was her regular labor coach (she'd insisted on it over Kass's numerous protests), but today she'd had to skip because of a conflict with a photo shoot for some new lipstick ad. Kass had tried to get her mother to fill in, but she had been tied up at the restaurant.

And so Kass was stuck with Kyle.

"Squeeze it all in . . . tight, tighter, tightest! . . . and then *releeeeease!*" Candy was saying animatedly. "Imagine that you're sitting on the toilet holding in your pee . . . and then *releeeeeasing!*"

Kyle's jaw dropped. "Seriously? Is she demented? Are all your classes like this?"

"Pretty much."

"Shit, remind me never to have a baby!"

"That's what I told myself, too, when I was your age."

"Really? I guess you changed your mind, then."

"Yeah, well, not exactly."

Kass continued squatting and squeezing and releasing, trying not to feel foolish. She reminded herself that it was necessary to condition herself mentally and physically—especially physically, and especially *down there*—for the rigors of childbirth. This was basically like studying for an econ exam or writing a thirty-page history paper. Kyle might not be into the spirit of things, but everyone else in the room was (i.e., six straight couples, two lesbian couples, and a gay male couple and their surrogate), so it was just a matter of feeding off all that happy expectant-couple energy.

For a brief moment Kass's thoughts wandered to Eduardo. When school started up again in mid-January, they didn't have any classes together, so she didn't see him for a while. She'd composed several long, rambling e-mails to him, trying to explain. But she never ended up sending them, hitting the delete button instead. After a while she stopped writing to him altogether.

She felt so bad about the way she'd treated him. She also missed him a lot. She missed his intellect. She missed his sweetness. She missed his beautiful face. She missed his lips . . .

She wished she had gone to San Diego with him that weekend.

She wished she had never passed that magazine stand the night Annabella was conceived.

She wished she hadn't waited so long to kiss him. If she hadn't, would things have turned out differently?

But that was in the past. There was no way they could resume their relationship. The last time she saw him—last month, around the middle of April—she'd run into him in front of the business school. She'd been wearing one of her anti-maternity-clothes T-shirts that revealed her belly in all its huge, farm-animal glory. He'd looked at it in shock, then met her gaze, his eyes full of surprise and hurt. She'd started to say something . . . but a couple of girls interrupted and whisked him away, jabbering about being late for their study group or whatever. She'd half expected him to text her or call her afterward. But he didn't. And she couldn't bring herself to call or text him either.

Because what would she say? *Eduardo, I'm so, so sorry for being such a psychotic, bipolar witch to you for so long. I don't even know how to explain what happened. See, I really, really liked you when we were going out fall semester, which is exactly what made me act like I didn't like you sometimes. And then that night, we were supposed to make love for the first time. It was going to be so amazing. But instead, there was this perfect storm of Really Bad Stuff, and I did the stupidest thing I've ever done in my entire life. That I'll ever do in my entire life. And then just before Christmas, I kissed you and made you think everything was okay between us. And then right after Christmas, I lied and told you I didn't want to see you anymore because I'd met another guy . . .*

"Kass? Yo! Snap out of your Kegel-orgasm-trance! Candygram says it's time to lie down on your back for our breathing exercises," Kyle told her.

"Oh!"

Kass reclined on the soft mat slowly, gingerly, using Kyle's arm for support. She had to stop thinking about Eduardo. And start focusing on the present. After all, she had a baby to deliver in less than three months.

"SO THANKS FOR FILLING IN AS MY LABOR COACH," KASS told Kyle over dinner at a pub in the neighborhood. "I know it's not exactly fun or interesting. And you probably had better things to do tonight."

"Nah, just catching up on the *Twilight Zone* marathon on Syfy," Kyle said, taking a sip of her chocolate milk shake. "There's like a zillion episodes. I swear, TiVo can be such a curse. Besides, the Candy Show was a blast. If I ever have to play a hippie-freak labor coach in a movie or whatever, I'll know who to channel."

Kass perked up. Kyle didn't generally express interest in much besides drinking and surfing the Internet and getting under their mother's skin. "Oh! So you're into acting now?" she said curiously.

"Nah, not really. I was just talking. So how are you doing, anyway? Are you peeing a lot? Waking up in the middle of the night?" She leaned forward and added, "Keeping in touch with your baby daddy?"

"Kyle, I told you before that—"

"I know what you told the fam. But it's me, *Kyle*. Your awesome little sister. You can trust me with anything. I won't tell, I promise."

Kass wasn't sure where this was coming from. Sure, she'd consumed a bathtub full of booze that night in November and spilled her guts to Kyle. But other than that, they didn't exactly have a sharing kind of relationship.

Kass picked up a bottle of ketchup and dumped it on her burger. "I don't really have anything to add," she said evasively. "I'm doing fine. Really. I finished up all my work for the semester, and I'm pretty sure I'll have a 4.0 going into my senior year. Kamille's moving into, uh, Chase's house after the wedding, so I'm going to turn her room into the nursery. Mom's been buying me tons of baby stuff, so I'm all set with that. She and Beau offered to subsidize my rent for the next year, so that'll be a big help. And I have some money saved up, too, from the restaurant and from birthday presents and savings bonds and all that."

"Uh-huh. That's superinteresting. *And?*"

"And . . . well . . . yeah, you're right, it's not easy, not being able to talk about the baby's father. I don't like keeping secrets. Especially from the people I love most in the world," Kass blurted out.

"Then why do you? Keep secrets, that is."

Kass sighed. "Because if I tell the truth, I'll end up hurting somebody. Really, really badly. Plus, everyone will hate me."

Kyle munched on a french fry and nodded thoughtfully. "Got it. But you know what, Kass? Secrets never stay secrets. The truth always comes out eventually. So, my advice? It's best to spill now versus later. That way, you're in control of the spin—not someone else who might distort the facts in a way that will make you seem even douchier than you already are."

"Oh! I hadn't thought of that!"

Kass grabbed a handful of french fries and stuffed them in her mouth. (Mmm. Maybe it was time she replaced her daily Oreo-and-ice-cream habit with a daily french-fry habit.) She thought about Kyle's words. The only two people who could possibly know about the baby's paternity were her and Chase. And because of Kass's brilliant DNA story, Chase thought the baby was someone else's, not his.

But. What if something unexpected happened (besides Chase putting two and two together, that is)? Like, what if Annabella was born with a medical condition that required genetic information from both parents . . . or, God forbid, some kind of transplant from a genetic match? Then Kass would be forced to confess the truth to Chase (and Kamille and the rest of her family) in the heat of the moment—a difficult, emotionally charged, possibly life-or-death moment—regardless of the consequences. Wouldn't it be better to come clean now, when the stakes weren't so high? And she, Kass, could be "in control of the spin" (as Kyle so artfully put it)?

On top of which . . . what if the tabloids got wind of the story? Kass wasn't sure how that could happen, but one never knew with them. They were relentless, they had resources, and they were evil. Pure evil. She knew personally, because they'd called her an ugly man or whatever. It would be disastrous if Kamille or anyone else read about Kass's drunken hookup with Chase on the Internet.

"Yeah, you should just tell me who the baby daddy is right

now," Kyle was saying. "It'll be off your conscience, then. And I can help you figure out what to say to Mom and Beau and stuff. I'm good at that."

"Yeah? Since when?"

"Since I started getting A's in school and all that bullshit. Mom thinks I walk on water now. She even said yes when I asked her for a loan so I could buy Uncle Desi's old Expedition. I gave her this whole made-up speech about how I was responsible enough to have my own car now, and how I wanted to keep honing my responsibility skills through long-term car ownership. That's the word I used, *honing*. And she actually believed me."

"Wow, that's comforting."

"Right? So you can trust me. I can help you."

"Let me think about it, okay?"

Kyle wagged a french fry in the air. "Okay. But don't think too long," she warned.

Kass frowned. Kyle's words reminded her of her *other* advice to Kass, last November. *Think less, hook up more.* That hadn't gone so well.

But maybe Kyle was right, this time? Maybe Kass shouldn't overanalyze the situation?

She grabbed more french fries. And flagged down the waitress for another order.

THIRTY-FIVE

KAMILLE

I DON'T THINK YOUR MOM LIKES ME VERY MUCH," Kamille told Chase. "She was giving off this weird vibe at the wedding shower."

The two of them were at Cartier on Rodeo Drive, checking out wedding bands. Hank and the crew were in the background, filming. They were the only people in the luxurious store, which made Kamille feel like royalty. She and Chase had looked at dozens of bands so far. It was hard to choose, especially since Kamille kept getting distracted by a gorgeous emerald necklace and matching earrings in a nearby case.

Maybe for our first anniversary, Kamille thought with a smile.

"No, babe, Mom *loves* you," Chase reassured her. "She's not always good at showing her feelings, that's all."

"Why, did she say something?"

"Yeah, she said we're a great couple. And she can't wait for lots and lots of grandchildren. Hey, check out this silver wedding band. Or is it platinum? What's the difference, anyway?"

"Platinum is way more valuable. And lasting. *And* it matches the amazing engagement ring you gave me." Kamille held up her left hand for him to see.

Chase took her hand in his and kissed each of her fingers tenderly. "Well, we're definitely going for platinum, then. Besides, you deserve the best. Always."

Kamille blushed. "You're so sweet."

"And you're my princess. I love you, babe."

"I love you, too."

Kamille wrapped her arms around his neck and hugged him tightly. In three weeks, they would be married. Mr. and Mrs. Chase Goodall. She couldn't wait!

The wedding plans were proceeding on schedule. Both the ceremony and reception would be at a dreamy oceanside resort in Rancho Palos Verdes. The minister from her family's church, Pastor Rodd, had agreed to marry them. Thanks to Courtney Powell, who was the world's most talented, together wedding planner, everything was set: the RSVPs, the flowers, the decorations, the music, the vows . . . all of it. And of course, there was Kamille's incredible Vera Wang dress. She had kept the design top secret, even from her mother. Courtney and Kass (and of course, Hank and the TV crew) were the only ones who had actually seen it so far.

It was going to be the happiest day of her life.

But first, she had to survive Chase's bachelor party. Which was happening this weekend.

"So. You looking forward to your big boy bash?" Kamille asked him casually. She had no idea what insanity Chase's friends had planned for him. Her own, relatively intimate bachelorette party was happening at the same time: a girls' trip to a Palm Springs resort with Kass, Kyle, their mother, and Simone.

"Honestly? I'd rather spend the weekend with you. In bed. If you know what I mean." Chase grinned.

Kamille gave him a look. She wished he wouldn't talk like that to her in front of the cameras. "Uh-huh. So where's the party going to be, anyway? Vegas? Or are you staying local?"

"No idea. Patrick and Dom and the other guys on the team have been planning it. And my brothers, too. Like, totally hush-hush stuff."

"Okay, well . . . try not to get *too* crazy."

"Babe, I'm already a married man as far as I'm concerned. I don't need these rings to tell me what I already know."

"What's that?"

"That I've got the most beautiful, fantastic girl in the world all to myself, and I am never going to do anything to screw that up. *Ever.*"

"Really?"

"Really. You can trust me."

Chase pulled her closer to him and kissed her on the lips. Kamille pressed her body against his, feeling his desire for her. They needed to go home. Immediately.

Besides, if she wore him out now, he would have nothing

left over for any lap-dancing skanks he might encounter this weekend.

THE BACHELORETTE PARTY WAS A DISASTER.

"Kat, you *must* see my surgeon, he's a miracle worker!" Pippa Ashton-Gould lay back on the poolside chaise longue, sipping a pomegranate margarita and eyeing the Speedo-clad waiters in a not-subtle way. "My va-jay-jay lips were practically hanging down to my knees!" she went on. "And it's not like I've had a dozen babies—just my darling Parker! *Anyhoo,* Dr. Marcelo cut off all that extra meat and now I'm as neat and trim as a virgin!" She spread her legs slightly and pushed the crotch part of her bikini bottoms to the side. "Here, let me show you what I'm—"

"*No!*" Kamille, Kass, and Kyle all shouted at the same time.

"Well, *I* want to see!" Simone said. She was so drunk that she'd taken off her bikini top and was drawing smiley faces on her boobs with a tube of lipstick.

"I want to see, too!" Kat agreed. She was almost as drunk as Simone, which was truly horrifying. Kamille hadn't seen her mother this wasted since that time several years ago when the three of them—Kat, Kamille, and Kass—had gone to a birthday party in Benedict Canyon. Kat drank too many cosmos, so Kass drove them all home via the twisty, windy canyon roads—but not before Kat threw up all over Kamille's brand-new shearling coat, which she'd bought herself for five hundred dollars saved up from an entire year of babysitting. Kamille had sobbed her eyes out and screamed at Kat for being "gross." Once they were home, Kat woke up Beau on the intercom (it was 3 A.M.) and told him that there was vomit all over the car. He dutifully got out of bed and cleaned it up so the acid wouldn't damage the interior.

Why had Kamille thought it was a good idea to have a bachelorette party with family members?

At least the resort pool was relatively deserted at this late hour—just a few couples trying to enjoy some romantic time (and who kept shooting their little group dirty looks) and an older guy who couldn't seem to take his eyes off Simone's bare boobs. (He was wearing a big, fat gold wedding ring; where was his wife?) Hank and the cameras were long gone. They had filmed all day—the fancy lunch, the lingerie gifts, the long afternoon of luxurious spa treatments—before driving back to L.A. Thank God. How embarrassing would that have been, seeing clips of Pippa blathering on about her labioplasty on the Life Network?

And why was Pippa even here? Kat had brought her along at the last minute, insisting that she needed *her* girlfriends at the party, too. "I'm sorry, Mommy, is this *your* bachelorette party?" Kamille had sniped at her. It was not a happy scene.

The party *really* hit rock bottom around midnight, when Pippa and Kat started teasing each other about their "double-decker bus" vaginas and having a contest to see whose was bigger by stuffing ice cubes into them. By the time Kamille left (or rather, ran out of there as fast as she could, pleading exhaustion), Kat was winning, with twelve cubes and counting. Kyle and Kass had excused themselves and gone up to their rooms long ago. Simone had disappeared, too, with the older, married guy who'd been checking out her boobs.

Hurrying through the ornate black-and-white Deco-style

lobby, trying to delete the last few awful hours from her memory, Kamille reminded herself to return to the beautiful resort sometime with Chase so she could actually *enjoy* herself. Chase was at his bachelor party now, wherever it was. She wondered if he was having fun. As long as he wasn't having *too* much fun . . . and as long as there weren't too many slores there. Kamille clenched her fists and forced herself to exhale. He'd said she could trust him. She wanted to believe him. She *had* to.

Back in the room Kamille was sharing with Kass, Kamille found her sister snoring away in bed, her big belly protruding like a small island under the elegant down cover. Kamille took off her flip-flops and lay down beside her.

"Kassie!" she whispered. "Kassie, are you awake?"

Kass's eyes flickered groggily. "Wha . . . ?" she mumbled.

"Oh, good, you're awake! How are you? Weren't Mommy and Pippa totally disgusting tonight?"

"Hmm."

"I mean, do we really need to hear about Pippa's droopy vag lips? And God, after you left, she was totally hitting on our waiter, who looked like he was about fourteen. Oh, and *God*, you wouldn't believe it, she and Mommy started stuffing ice cubes up their—"

"Ew, shut up!" Kass lifted her head and glanced around. "What time is it, anyway?"

"I don't know. One, one-thirty? Anyway, I wish this was a cozier bachelorette party—like, just you and me and Simone. We could have gone to Vegas or something. Hey, maybe we still could?"

"Me partying in Vegas, that's hilarious," Kass said sarcastically. "Besides, there's no way in hell I'd spend an entire week-end with you and Simone. The only reason I came today was because Kyle and Mom were here, too."

"I know Simone can be a bitch sometimes," Kamille said. "And I know she can be kind of . . . um, nuts." She thought about the peeing incident at Hyde. "But she's a lot of fun! And she's one of my oldest friends."

"Whatever. I can't stand being in the same room with her."

"I know. But try to make an effort, okay? For the wedding?"

Kass didn't reply. She gazed up at the ceiling and stroked her belly.

"Is he . . . kicking?" Kamille asked her curiously.

"Yes. What makes you think it's a he?"

"You're my sister. I know everything about you. Can I touch him?"

"I guess?"

Kamille placed her hand on Kass's stomach. Nothing. Still nothing.

Then, all of a sudden . . .

"Ohmigod!" Kamille cried out. It was the most amazing thing she had ever felt. A gentle rolling sensation, like waves undulating under Kass's skin, followed by a pounding, puls-ing kick. "There he is! Oh my God, it's incredible! He's doing jujitsu!"

"Actually, I'm kinda thinking *he* might be a *she,*" Kass ad-mitted.

"Really?"

"Really. I had this dream that she was a girl."

"Ohmigod, how cool is that?" Kamille nestled closer to Kass. "It's all so miraculous. Isn't it? All this? I mean, last year this time, we were just . . . I don't know, *us*. And now you're having a baby . . . and I'm getting married . . ."

"Yeah. Miraculous," Kass said quietly.

Kamille reached for Kass's hand and squeezed it tightly. "Promise me something? That no matter what, and no matter how busy and crazy things get, we'll still be sisters? And best friends?"

Kass squeezed Kamille's hand back. "I promise," she whispered. "But you have to promise, too. No matter what."

"No matter what. I love you, doll."

"I love you, too, doll."

Kamille closed her eyes and felt herself melting into sleep, her head cradled against Kass's shoulder. It was the most peaceful and contented she'd been in . . . forever.

THIRTY-SIX

KASS

THE WHITE DOVE INN WAS A ZOO. HANK AND HIS TV crew were everywhere, setting up the lights and cameras and other equipment. The caterers were rushing around with bottles of wine, buckets of ice, and numerous trays of whatever. The wedding planner, a terrifyingly efficient woman named Courtney Powell (whom Kass had met a couple of times before), was ordering around her team of cowering assistants on her hair-thin silver headset.

And speaking of doves, there was a cage of them somewhere, waiting to be released once Kamille and Chase declared "I do." (That had been the network's idea.)

It was a gray, foggy day. June gloom. That's what SoCalers called the overcast weather that was typical for this time of year. Kass felt it inside, too, the gloom. She told herself to snap out of it, already; it was almost showtime, after all.

Standing in the first-floor parlor alone (Kamille had sent her to find a safety pin, and Kass had decided to take a brief mental health break, to collect her thoughts), she gazed outside of the window, at the first guests who were beginning to gather on the lawn. There was Kamille's agent, Giles Sinclair, talking on his phone. (The guy was *always* on a call.) There was Pippa, dressed in a skintight minidress that came up almost to her crotch. (Well, at least she'd had that labioplasty procedure.) There were random Romeros and Fergusons, including some out-of-town cousins and aunts and uncles Kass hadn't seen in forever.

And there was Chase's mom (who seemed freaky and repressed, like a character out of an Alfred Hitchcock movie) and his sister, Amanda (ditto). Chase's dad, next to them, was tall and broad-shouldered, a middle-aged version of his oldest son. He had been at the rehearsal dinner last night, telling a bunch of jokes about brides on their wedding night and consuming an alarming amount of alcohol without ever appearing to be drunk.

It occurred to Kass, not for the first time, that Mr. and Mrs. Goodall were Annabella's biological grandparents. Not that they would ever know it, but still. Kass adored her own grandparents, the Romeros and the Fergusons (and also Beau's parents, who had flown out from New Orleans for the wedding). Her relationship with all of her grandparents had always been so important to her. It was sad, thinking that Annabella would have only Kat and Beau.

Kass also prayed that whatever crazy, alcoholic, or other

bad genes the Goodalls possessed would not show up in Annabella's perfect little brain and body.

As for Chase . . . well, Kass had come *this close* to telling Kamille the truth about the baby. Several times, in fact, ever since she'd had that talk with Kyle after the Lamaze class.

But she hadn't been able to go through with it. She loved Kamille too much. Kamille seemed incredibly happy with Chase lately, far less of the dysfunctional drama-queen girlfriend than she used to be.

And Chase seemed to have cleaned up his act? Maybe? The same weekend that Kamille had her bachelorette party in Palm Springs, Chase had apparently (and very publicly) left his party in Vegas *early,* declaring that his bachelor days were behind him. The press was all over that one, saying that he had been "reformed" by "true love" or whatever.

Kass wasn't sure how long the media honeymoon was going to last. More important, she wasn't sure if Chase's changed-man act was for real—or permanent.

But whatever the case, Kamille deserved a chance with him. And today, she deserved to enjoy the dream wedding that she had waited for so long.

Kass's cell buzzed. It was a text from Kamille.

KASSIE WHERE R U???? DID U FIND A SAFETY
PIN???? COME BACK TO THE ROOM I NEED U TO
HELP ME WITH MY DRESS!!!!

Kass sighed and tucked her cell into her bag. She left the parlor and headed down the hall.

She ran into Kat outside the dining room, looking lovely

in her royal-blue mother-of-the-bride dress. (She'd bought six different mother-of-the-bride dresses and finally settled on this one, this morning.) She was giving one of the caterers a hard time about the passed hors d'oeuvres. "I don't care what Courtney told you! The beef absolutely *has* to be medium rare, and it absolutely *has* to be served at room temperature!" she was saying in her scary don't-fuck-with-me voice.

Kat paused and waved to Kass. "Hey, honey, you need anything?" she said sweetly, suddenly switching to Helpful Mom mode.

"I'm good, Mom, thanks. I'm heading up to see Kamille. Hey, do you know where Bree is? I need to go over her flower-girl routine with her one more time."

"I think she and Kyle are up there with Kamille."

"'Kay, thanks."

Kass proceeded down the hall toward the staircase. The girls' dressing room (for Kamille, Kass, Kyle, Bree, and Simone) was on the second floor; the boys' (for Chase, Benjy, Beau, and Chase's brothers, Zach and Justin) was on the ground floor. Kamille had been fanatical about Chase not seeing her before the ceremony. She had been equally fanatical about having only her bridal party see her dress. Not even Kat knew what it looked like.

Kass's own dress, she had to admit, was pretty perfect. Kamille had insisted on a pale pink gossamer silk, which complemented Kass's light brown hair and hazel eyes, and the Empire waist, which made her enormous belly look . . . well, not so enormous. Kass had even agreed to an updo and full makeup for the occasion. It *was* kind of nice feeling so put-together—glamorous, even—after so many months of self-induced, pregnant-girl frumpiness.

As Kass neared the stairs, she could hear violins warming up from somewhere in the inn, playing the opening strains of Pachelbel's Canon. The ceremony would be starting in less than an hour.

And soon after that, Kamille would become Mrs. Chase Goodall.

"Cut it out! Someone's gonna see us!"

Kass stopped in her tracks. The giddy female voice was coming from somewhere nearby.

"Yeah, but check out this bad boy. What am I supposed to do with that? Huh?" a guy replied teasingly.

"Hold it in your pants till afterward. Maybe during the reception?"

Kass frowned. *What the hell?*

She backed up, slowly, quietly. She realized that the voices were coming from the coat-check room.

She craned her neck and peered inside the dimly lit space . . .

. . . and saw Chase leaning against the wall, running his soon-to-be-married hands all over Simone's Pilates-toned butt.

Kass clamped her hand over her mouth to keep from screaming.

And then she turned and made her escape, before the world's most duplicitous asshole (correction: world's most duplicitous assholes, *plural*) noticed her.

"KAM, I HAVE TO TALK TO YOU. *RIGHT NOW.*"

"What?" Kamille turned around and held up two pairs of earrings. "Kassie, do you think I should wear Grandma

Romero's pearl ones? Or Grandma Ferguson's sapphire ones? I need something old, something new, something borrowed, and something blue, right? So if I wear the sapphire ones, I can knock off the old, borrowed, *and* blue at the same time. God, this is complicated!"

"Kassie, where've you been? Do you like my hair? Ky let me borrow her straightening-er!" Bree squealed happily.

Bree looked adorable in her rose-colored flower-girl dress. Kyle looked pretty, too, in her pale pink bridesmaid's dress. Kass wished they could all sit around admiring one another's dresses and hair and makeup and enjoying this fun, special, girlie time. But unfortunately, that wasn't going to happen.

"Kyle and Bree, can you excuse Kamille and me for a moment? We need some privacy," Kass said tersely.

"Why, so you can give her some advice about her wedding night?" Kyle joked. "I think Chase's dad already covered that at the rehearsal dinner."

"Huh?" Bree looked confused. "What are you guys *talking* about?"

Kass clenched her fists. "Please. Kyle, just two minutes. Can you take Bree and get a soda or something?"

"Fine!" Kyle took Bree's arm and led her out into the hall. "Normally, Brie Cheese, I'd say that someone's plugging right now. Except we all know that Kass can't be plugging . . ."

"Huh?"

Once they were gone, Kamille lit into Kass. "You *know* Bree and Kyle can't eat or drink anything with their dresses on! They might get a stain! Besides, what's so important that it can't wait? Did you get my safety pin? Plus, I really, really need your help with this damned zipper, I think it's—"

"You can't marry Chase," Kass cut in.

"Ha-ha, very funny. Seriously, this zipper is driving me insane."

"I just caught him making out with Simone. In the coat-check room. Kam, I'm so sorry, but he's a cheater, and he always will be."

Kamille's jaw dropped. Then she crossed her arms over her chest. "I'm gonna take a deep breath and forget you ever said that."

"Kamille—"

"Actually, no! I'm *not* gonna forget you ever said that. You need to hear the truth!"

"No! You don't under—"

"Shut up, I'm talking! You've always been jealous of me, haven't you? And now it's worse than ever because I have this incredible, amazing modeling career that's gonna make me superfamous, and this incredible, amazing fiancé who's about to become my husband, who's *already* superfamous. And you? You're fat and pregnant and you don't have a husband . . . or a boyfriend, even. And at the rate you're going, you're probably never *gonna* have a boyfriend or a husband. Well, I'm sorry if your life sucks! I'm sorry you're alone! But it's not my fault, and it's completely psychotic of you to make up shit about Simone, who you've always hated, and Chase, just so you can feel better about—"

"Chase is the baby's father," Kass blurted out.

Dead silence.

"Did you hear me, Kam? I'm so, so sorry, but Chase is the baby's father. Back in November? That night you broke the martini pitcher or whatever? See, I, uh, got insanely drunk on tequila because I'd had this fight with Eduardo." Kass decided not to throw Kyle under the bus about the tequila part; otherwise their mother might lock her up and throw away the key. "And I came home to our house, and Chase was there," she went on. "I think he was drunk, too. I didn't even know what was happening; I thought he was Eduardo, that's how out of it I was. Anyway, we, uh . . . you know . . . and then, on Christmas day, I did a home pregnancy test and—"

Kamille crossed the distance between her and Kass in two quick strides and slapped her, hard.

"Ow!" Kass cried out. "What'd you do that for?"

"For being a fucking *liar*! And a *witch*! How *dare* you make up this psychotic story about Chase?"

Kass touched her cheek. It stung like hell. "Why would I make up something like that, Kam? I've been tearing myself up inside wondering if I should tell you or not. I didn't want to hurt you. But after I saw him downstairs with . . . anyway, I had to tell you, before it was too late."

"You're *deranged*! I'm telling Mommy and Beau; they're gonna throw your lying, psychotic ass into a *mental* institution!"

The door creaked open ever so slightly. Suddenly Kass realized that they were not alone.

A TV cameraman was standing in the doorway, filming.

"Get the hell *out* of here!" Kamille screamed at him. "This is private! Don't you vultures have anything better to do?"

The door opened wider. The cameraman stepped aside, and Simone walked in, smoothing the skirt of her dress. "Yo, bitches! What'd I miss? Sounds like someone needs a Valium," she called out cheerfully. "Hey, I saw a bunch of photographers outside. What do you say we go out there and give them some crotch shots?" She giggled.

Kass glanced quickly at Kamille. Kamille fake-smiled at Simone. "Kassie was telling me that she just saw you and Chase downstairs," she said coldly.

Simone blinked. "I don't think so. I've been out back for the last half hour, um, smoking a cigarette with your sister Kyle."

Kass gasped at the lie. Kamille turned away for a second. Then her face grew hard with fury, and she slapped Simone, too.

Simone began crying. "What the *fuck,* Kamille?" she whimpered.

"I never want to see either of you two sorry bitches ever again," Kamille announced.

And then she stormed out the door, shoving the cameraman aside roughly, and disappeared down the hall in a cloud of ivory silk.

THIRTY-SEVEN

KAMILLE

"KAM, WAIT! PLEASE, LET'S TALK ABOUT THIS!"

Kamille heard Kass behind her, following. That slore Simone wasn't even bothering. Hopefully, she was crawling home in shame like the rat that she was. Or jumping out of the second-floor window and plummeting to her death. Either was fine with Kamille, she could give a shit.

Word about the incident must have spread like wildfire, though, because Kamille spotted two more cameramen up ahead, filming her as she headed in their direction. Fuck it. She didn't care anymore. Let the TV viewers, let the entire fucking world, see what deceitful, lying sluts her ex-sister and her ex-friend were.

"Kamille, what's going on?" Her mother had appeared out

of nowhere, carrying a sewing kit and a lint remover. She fell in step beside her. "Why are you out here in your dress? Oh my goodness, it's beautiful! It's exactly what I would have picked out for you! That Vera Wang is a genius! But, honey? Did you know your zipper's undone? And the guests are starting to arrive, and they'll see you, and why do you look all red in the face, like you're about to kill somebody? Is it the caterers? Because they were kind of making me mad, too, but I think I straightened out the problem with the Thai beef skewers—"

"Mom, shut *up*!" Kamille barreled ahead of her.

"Kamille! Sweetheart! What's going on? Are you having cold feet, or—"

"Ask your whore daughter Kassidy, she's right behind us."

"What?"

"You heard me."

Kamille started down the stairs without waiting for a response. She remembered to pick up her long skirt, but a second too late; she heard a loud ripping noise as her heel caught on the hem. Whatever.

"Kamille!"

"Kamille, wait!"

"Kamille, can you slow down, we're having a hard time framing this shot!"

Now the entire entourage was following her: her mother, Kass, Courtney, and what seemed like most of the TV crew. Hank and the network must be getting some killer footage, she thought darkly.

As she approached the boys' dressing room on the first floor, she heard Chase and the others laughing and joking about something. She pushed the door open and marched inside.

They were all in there, dressed in their elegant gray-and-black tuxedos: Chase, Beau, Benjy, and Chase's brothers. Benjy, Zach, and Justin were sitting cross-legged on the bed, playing a video game on somebody's iPad. Beau was adjusting the knot on Chase's tie. Two cameramen were already set up and filming; they'd obviously gotten the word.

Chase stood there, looking more gorgeous than ever in his tux. He wore a single cream rose at his lapel—just like the cream roses he'd given Kamille after their very first fight, when they'd told each other "I love you" for the very first time.

But at this moment the memory of those roses was doing nothing for Kamille. She wished she had a knife . . . so she could cut off his wretched little penis and watch him writhe and scream in agony.

"Babe? You look amazing! But you're not supposed to let me see you," Chase said, his blue eyes bewildered.

"You okay, sweetheart? You want me to get your mom for you?" Beau said, sounding concerned.

Kamille wriggled her engagement ring off her finger. She started to throw it at Chase . . . then changed her mind.

"No, actually, I'm not gonna give this back to you so you can return it to the store and spend the money on Simone or Kassie or one of your other girlfriends," she announced. "I'm gonna keep it and spend the money on myself. Yeah, I'll buy some billboard space on Sunset, *babe,* so the entire city of Los Angeles can know what a fucking *man-whore,* what a fucking *con job* you are. Or I might take out a contract on your head. Whatever. I've got lots of time to think about it, now that I don't have this bullshit sham of a wedding to go through. *Fuck* you, Chase! I hope you rot in *hell.*"

All the color had drained out of Chase's face. "Kamille? Babe? I don't understand where this is coming from. Could we just go somewhere alone and—"

"No! You're wasting my time, douche bag. Oh, and by the way? About Simone? She did tell you about her herpes and all her other STDs, right? Better get yourself to a doctor. 'Kay, bye for now! Have a nice life!" Air-kissing, Kamille turned and walked away from Chase.

This time, for good.

PART V

THE FAMILY THAT GIVES BIRTH TOGETHER . . .

THIRTY-EIGHT

KYLE

L.A. WAS ALWAYS A BITCH IN AUGUST, BUT THIS YEAR SEEMED worse than usual. As Kyle drove to the party in Laurel Canyon in her new (well, technically used) Expedition that she'd bought from Uncle Desi, she cranked up the a/c to the max. She rolled down the windows at the same time, too. Doing eighty-five on the 101, one could generate a killer breeze.

Her cell buzzed. It was a text from Ash:

WHERE U B, HO?

Nice. Kyle picked up her phone and dialed. Ash answered immediately.

"Why're you calling, that's weird," Kyle heard Ash yell, over what sounded like screeching guitars and a whole lot of cheering and a girl shouting: "Who wants my panties?"

"Yeah, talking on the phone's so 2008. I didn't feel like typing, 'kay? I'll be there in a few minutes. Do I need to pick up Priscilla?"

"Nah, she's here already, sucking some guy's—"

There was a peal of laughter, and a scream, and more laughter. Then the phone went dead.

Fun party, Kyle thought. *Better get there quick so I don't miss out.*

She pushed the accelerator down with just her big right toe and watched the needle climb to eighty-six . . . eighty-eight . . . ninety. It *was* ninety, right? Her vision was a little blurry from the vodka shots she'd had before heading out. But she was basically fine to drive. And besides, she'd had a tough day today—nothing good on TV, and her mother had been a complete bitch to her about cleaning her room.

It was also the four—no, five-year—anniversary of her father's death. Not that Kyle believed in anniversaries, which were kind of bullshit. Still, under the circumstances, she was entitled to as many vodka shots as she wanted.

Frankly, she was entitled to as many vodka shots as she wanted *every* day, not just today, considering how much stupid drama her family had been putting her through lately. Kass's baby-daddy bomb, the epic wedding fail . . . and Kass and Kamille weren't speaking to each other, which meant that the rest of the family had to walk on eggshells constantly. And of course, the fucking tabloids had been all over all of them since June, and even more since mid-July, when the Life Network had aired the now-infamous "Kamille and Chase" episode.

The worst moment was when Kyle caught Bree watching it

on Hulu, even though Kat and Beau had forbidden her. Poor Bree, who had been sheltered from the truth on the big day, had sobbed her eyes out . . .

Kyle finally reached the address in Laurel Canyon and parked behind a long row of BMWs, Benzes, and other fancy rides. It was only five-ish—still daylight. Ash had texted her earlier that the party had been going since noon, starting at the pool and spreading its tentacles inside and up as the day progressed. Kyle had worn her turquoise bikini, black cover-up, and no shoes. She'd forgotten to put on makeup—but at this point, everyone at the party was probably too drunk or high or both to care about nuances like lip gloss and eyeliner. She never had a problem hooking up at these things, anyway.

"Kyle!" Ash greeted her at the door as though she owned the place. She was wearing a red satin demi and supershort shorts and waving a cloudy-looking bong in the air. "Where the fuck you been?"

"Uh, hey."

"Come on, lemme introduce you to"—Ash turned to the two guys standing behind her—*"what* did you say your name was?"

"I'm Elmo, and this is Cookie Monster," the first guy said with a straight face.

"Ha-ha, good one, dude! Yeah, I'm Cookie Monster, and I wanna eat your cookies!"

They started fist-pumping.

Kyle frowned. She would need a *lot* more shots, not to mention the rest of that bong, if she was going to hook up with the likes of these two losers. There had to be higher-quality meat at this party. Or maybe she would skip the whole tedious mating ritual and just get wasted. (*More* wasted, that is.) Over the years, she'd cultivated the art of numbing out in various ways. But in the end, it was all the same: hooking up, drinking, smoking pot, whatever. Any of it was better than feeling stuff.

She'd actually been doing better for a while, not needing the booze or the pot or the rest of it, partly due to Benjy, who had become a good friend. It was nice to have someone not completely lame who understood her, and who didn't judge her or patronize her (like her mom most of the time, plus her teachers at school *all* of the time).

But Kyle and Benjy's friendship had kind of cooled over the summer, after Kamille's disastrous nonwedding. He had convinced Kyle to try out for Mr. Weaver's play at the community center; she'd signed up for an audition slot, only to blow it off at the last minute for no particular reason. And then she'd started breaking into the parents' liquor cabinet again, and smoking a little pot here and there. She was also hanging out with Ash and Priscilla more and more, even scoring an updated fake ID so she could go to college bars with them. Benjy had noticed and tried to get her to talk about it. Which had the opposite effect, making her want to *not* talk about it. After a while he stopped trying, until finally, they were back to the old days of barely speaking to each other.

Whatever. She didn't care anymore. She was here now, at this party, and she wanted to forget it all. Benjy, her mom, her dead dad, her whole stupid, fucking life.

Sighing, she followed Ash and her bong inside the house. The *Sesame Street* duo had wandered off to hit on two girls who looked *way* too young to be here. Once in the living room, Kyle could barely make out the confusing tangle of bodies: naked, half naked, dancing, lap-dancing, inhaling, not inhaling. There were pitchers of beer everywhere, likely laced with quaaludes, and garbage cans filled with jungle juice, fruit floating on the top. The coffee table was covered with a fine layer of white powder, and the air reeked of pot.

"Ohmigod, *Kyyyyyllllle!*" Priscilla bounced up to her and gave her a slobbery French kiss. "Mmm, you taste like an Altoid!" she said breathlessly.

Kyle pulled back. "And you taste like stale pizza. *Ew.* What the fuck, Priscilla?"

"Ash, did you give Kyle her birthday present yet?" Priscilla asked their friend.

"Huh? My birthday was like months ago," Kyle said.

"It's a *belated* birthday present, idiot, 'cause we forgot to get you anything for your *real* birthday." Ash reached into her short-shorts pocket and pulled out a tiny white, heart-shaped tablet. She pressed it against Kyle's lips. "Happy Birthday!"

"Um, what is it?"

"Don't think about it too much. Just swallow," Ash advised her.

Kyle hesitated. She wanted to get wasted, sure, but she usually liked to know what she was taking first. "But what's in it?" she persisted.

Priscilla stroked her cheek. "Kyle, puh-lease, you're gonna love it!"

"Come on, bitch, don't be shy," Ash urged.

Kyle was about to just go along with it—what the hell?— when she heard an insistent buzzing sound. Was that someone's phone? Was that *her* phone? Maybe someone was texting her? She managed to find her cell, which she had apparently wedged into her bikini top (she couldn't remember when), and glanced at the screen. There were three voice-mail messages from home. When had all those calls come in?

Kyle plucked the little white pill from Ash and held it tightly in her palm as she listened to the first message. It was from Bree.

"Hey, Ky? Where are you? Can you come home right away? 'Cause I think I'm sick, and there's no one here. And I might be in big trouble, too, 'cause I saw you drinking that stuff today, Grey Moose, and I don't know why you like it because it tastes like *yech*. Anyway, I got it out of Mommy and Daddy's bottle closet, and I tried some, but then I accidentally spilled it all over the floor, and now Mommy and Daddy are prolly gonna be supermad. And I think I've got the flu, 'cause I just threw up . . ."

"Jesus." Kyle hung up and dialed the home number. There was no answer. She also tried Bree's cell. No answer there either.

She checked the other two messages. They were also from Bree, basically saying the same stuff.

"Kyle, come *on*!" Ash was tugging on her arm impatiently. "Stop checking your fucking messages!"

"I've gotta go."

"*What?*" Ash and Priscilla said in unison.

"I've gotta go. Here's your present back. Sorry."

Kyle ran, or tried to run, through the jam-packed room, the sweaty crush of bodies. It was all her fault. She must have left the liquor cabinet unlocked. *God*, she was an idiot.

"DON'T YOU EVER, EVER TOUCH THAT STUFF AGAIN. DO you hear me? *Ever!*"

Bree stared up at her guiltily. She was lying in her ruffly pink princess bed, clutching her teddy bear to her chest. Kyle had found her there when she got home. Thank *God*. It could have been so much worse . . . like, Bree could have OD'd on alcohol, or fallen into the pool and drowned, or wandered into busy traffic, or—

"I'm so sorry, Ky!" Bree squeaked. "I feel a lot better now. The ice water helped, and the tummy medicine, and the cold cloth on my forehead."

"Good. How much of the, uh, Grey Moose did you drink?"

"I don't know. I tried to drink as much as you did. But it tasted so awful!"

Kyle groaned. "So you were spying on me before?"

"No. I don't know. Maybe." Bree looked away, blushing.

"Brie Cheese, we've gotta have a talk about that. First of all, you shouldn't copy whatever I do. 'Cause in this case, I made a mistake. A stupid mistake. I shouldn't have touched Mom and Dad's, I mean *your* dad's, bottle of vodka. Or any of those bottles. They're supposed to be locked up in the bottle closet, it's called the liquor cabinet, and they're only for adults. Not for kids."

"But *you're* not a kid!"

"Yes, I am. I'm a big kid, almost an adult, but I'm technically still a kid. I'm seventeen. And even adults don't know how to handle that stuff sometimes." Kyle wanted to add, *Like your mom, Angie*. But she bit her tongue.

"Well, I'm never drinking that Grey Moose again, 'cause it tastes bad, and it made me feel horrible," Bree declared.

"What the *hell*, Kyle?"

Kyle turned around. Benjy was standing in the doorway, looking seriously pissed.

"What's this about Bree drinking vodka?" he demanded angrily. "And what's up with the empty bottle on the living room floor? Have you been getting my sister *drunk*, you self-destructive asshole? She's *eleven*."

"No, no! I've been out this whole time," Kyle said quickly. "See, she got into the parents' liquor cabinet, and that was kinda my bad because I left it unlocked. But she's fine now, and we've been having a nice talk about it, and—"

"*What* in the name of God is going on?"

Kat stormed into Bree's room, followed by Beau. Kyle cringed. Her mother, wearing a pretty white suit (probably from a visit to her father's grave), looked like she was ready to kill someone—well, *her*. So did Beau.

She was so screwed.

THIRTY-NINE

KAMILLE

KAMILLE OPENED HER CLOSET DOOR AND RAN HER fingers over the row of dresses. The cucumber mask on her face was dry, and the thirty minutes were almost up on her teeth-whitening strips. She sipped her glass of champagne—one of her standard pre-glam rituals—and bobbed her head to Beyoncé's "Beautiful Liar," which was playing on her CD player.

Hmm, should she go with the Azzedine Alaïa? Or the Chanel? Giles had mentioned that tonight's movie premiere, at Mann's Chinese Theatre, would be especially celebrity studded, and there was going to be a reporter from *Vogue* there who'd asked to meet her. She finally settled on the Chanel, which she'd spent a small fortune on.

She plucked the filmy wine-red dress off its hanger and draped it across her king-size bed. She loved her new apartment on Westmount Drive, which was spacious in every way—big, airy rooms, massive closets, tall ceilings. It was so much better than the overcrowded family house in Los Feliz. Or the cramped little bungalow she'd shared with the sister-who-shall-not-be-named, until two months ago.

Or Chase's place. That was probably her favorite thing about this apartment. There was no Chase in it. No assholes, *period.*

For a while after that disastrous day in June, Chase had actually tried to get in touch with her, wanting to "explain things." What a jerk. Kamille had ignored the countless messages, texts, and e-mails, and she'd tossed the three dozen cream roses with their pathetic "I'm sorry" note into the trash compactor.

Giles had come to the rescue, lining her up with a publicist to deal with the media aftermath. Including the humiliating *Happily Ever After* episode that had aired last month on the Life Network, showing absolutely *everything.*

And somehow, miraculously, Kamille had come out on top. The magazines had portrayed her (rightly) as the innocent victim. The glut of publicity even ended up helping her professionally because suddenly, overnight, everyone in the country knew who she was. Giles had even managed to book her first cover, for *Mademoiselle,* as well as a guest spot on a wildly popular reality dance contest on one of the major networks. So really, her career was better than ever now.

As for Kass . . . they hadn't spoken since the wedding. The nonwedding. Kamille had arranged through her mother and Beau to come to Sunday Night Dinner every other week, and insisted that Kass be there on the alternate Sundays only. Kat

had tried to play peacemaker, among other things informing
Kamille that Chase had actually committed a crime against
Kass because she had been too drunk to give consent. She
said she'd even tried to convince Kass to press charges for date
rape, but that Kass had refused because she wanted to "move
on." Whatever. It was Kass's fault for getting so wasted to begin
with. She *knew* she couldn't handle alcohol; she shouldn't have
put herself in that position. Kamille had zero sympathy. And
why was her mother being so understanding about it, instead
of disowning Kass's sorry ass?

But enough about Kass. Kamille had to get ready for
the party. Really, her life had less and less to do with her
family these days, which was just fine with her. She, too, was
moving on.

Kamille wandered into the bathroom, which was brand-
new and all white with floor-to-ceiling mirrors. The dressing-
room-style lighting was at once flattering and precise, which
meant that she could apply her makeup perfectly—and also
scrutinize back zits, excess body hair, and so forth without
feeling *too* ugly.

She scrutinized herself now. Perfect.

The phone rang just as Kamille was spraying herself with
J'Adore perfume. She glanced at the screen; it was her mother.

She almost let it go to voice mail, then changed her mind
at the last second and picked up. "Hi, Mommy, I really can't
talk right now, I'm getting ready for that big movie premiere I
told you about," she said quickly. "At Mann's Chinese?" She
ran a clean washcloth under warm water and started removing her cucumber mask, hoping her mother would be suitably
impressed by her very glamorous plans.

"Hi, doll. I won't keep you. I just . . . listen, could Kyle come stay with you for a few days?"

"*Excuse* me?"

"We had an incident tonight. I can explain more later, but long story short, she broke into the liquor cabinet and helped herself to some vodka. But the worst part is, she left the house without locking it back up again, and Bree ended up, well, helping herself to the vodka, too. And getting sick."

"Ohmigod, are you serious?"

"I'm afraid so."

"Is Bree okay?"

"It depends on what you mean by *okay*, but yes, she's fine."

Kyle! What an idiot. Kamille flashed back to when Kyle had been busted for showing Bree how to roll a joint. Kamille wasn't exactly a saint herself, and she'd done some pretty stupid stuff when she was a teenager, too.

But not *that* stupid. All her drinking (and occasional pot smoking, and that one time she'd tried E with Jeremy Weinstein) had taken place at her friends' houses, with parents safely out of town (or better yet, out of the country) and the nanny cams on the off position. And she'd never, ever exposed any of her younger sibs to that kind of behavior.

"Beau and I need some alone time with Bree so we can talk to her, get her back to normal," her mother was saying. "I promise, it'll just be a few days. Or a week or two, tops. Once school starts, we'll be back to our usual routine here, anyway. Kyle will be too busy with homework to get into trouble, and same with Bree."

Kamille wasn't so sure about the "too busy" part, especially with respect to Kyle. "But, Mommy, I've got a big shoot coming up," she complained. "Remember that bathing-suit ad I told you about? And Giles has me going to all these events at night. I can't babysit Kyle twenty-four/seven!"

"I'm not asking you to do that, sweetheart. Just let her crash on your lovely new sofa bed that Beau and I bought for you. And if you have any liquor there, please lock it up! *Double* lock it!"

"But, Mommy—"

"Oops, that's . . . uh, that's my other line. I've gotta go, doll. I'll call you back later, okay?"

"But, Mommy, I—"

The connection went dead.

"Shit!" Her superspacious apartment was about to get a lot less spacious.

Kamille went back to removing her cucumber mask, muttering in annoyance to herself. A couple of minutes later, the phone rang again. It was her mother, *again*. This time, she decided to let it go to voice mail. She didn't want to hear about any more family drama, and she really did have to get out the door . . .

A box popped up on the screen, letting her know that she had a new voice-mail message. A second later, a text popped up below it. From her mother.

It said:

KASS JUST CALLED SHES AT THE HOSPITAL SHES IN LABOR

For a moment Kamille just stood there frozen in place, staring at the text message. Then the shock turned into something else: the old rage, stirring up inside of her and making her want to throw things. Kass was finally going to have her baby. *Chase's* baby. A child that would remind Kamille forever of just how low people could go, how no one could be trusted.

Not even family.

But enough of the pity party. She had a *real* party to get ready for. Kamille took a deep breath, then reached into her makeup box and grabbed her favorite red YSL lipstick.

FORTY

KYLE

Lying in bed, Kyle wondered why she couldn't stop crying. She hadn't cried like this since she was four, when she forgot her pink, blue, and lavender kiki that Grandma Romero had made for her at Disneyland. Her father had driven back there, alone, after closing, and talked a security guard into letting him onto the grounds. He'd finally found the baby blanket near the Mad Hatter's Tea Cups, covered in someone's red slushie, and brought it home.

Kyle sniffed and blew her nose. What was wrong with her? Why couldn't she pull herself together? She wondered if she still had a small stash of Xanax hidden in her underwear drawer, which had been Ash and Priscilla's birthday present to her *last* year . . .

There was a knock on her door. Benjy poked his head in. "Can I come in?"

Kyle sat up abruptly and drew her kiki around her. "Why, so you can yell at me some more?"

Benjy walked into the room and sat down cross-legged on her bed. He gazed intently at her face.

"What?" Kyle snapped. "Why are you staring me?"

"You've got a giant booger hanging down—right there," he said, pointing.

"Gee, thanks." Kyle grabbed a tissue and blew her nose again.

"You okay?"

"No, I'm not okay. I feel like shit."

"Bree's downstairs eating an enormous bowl of mint chocolate-chip ice cream, if that makes you feel any better. With chocolate syrup and a mountain of that fake whipped cream."

"Really?" Kyle was relieved. But only slightly. "I've like totally fucked her up for life," she rambled on miserably. "She's like this sweet, innocent kid, and now she thinks it's cool to drink vodka, like me. Like her goddamned 'hero.'" She added, "Plus, Mom's kicking me out of the house."

"What? Tell me."

"She said I have to go live with Kamille for a while, or something. I guess she hates me and she doesn't want me around anymore."

Benjy regarded her. "Look. Kyle. Nobody hates you. And you haven't ruined Bree for life; she'll recover. As for her thinking that drinking's cool . . . it's probably the opposite. The stuff made her sick. Maybe it's even a *good* thing that she knows how gross booze is, this young, so she won't end up like . . ." He hesitated.

"Like me?"

"I was actually thinking about our mom. But yeah, like you, too. 'Cause you did screw up, big-time. I don't know what you were thinking. Frankly, I don't know what you've been thinking for months, now. You were acting like a human being for a while, and then after the whole Kamille-and-Chase thing, you kind of lost it again."

"Yeah, I know." Kyle buried her face in her hands. "It's just that . . . everything got so fucked up with this family, and stressful, and I just don't know how to deal with that."

"So you thought that going into self-destruct mode was a good idea?"

Kyle shook her head. "No! Well, yes! Maybe! I don't know." She took a deep breath, trying to express all the complicated, jumbled-up feelings she'd kept buried for so long. "See, it's like when my dad died," she began. "I never told anyone this, but when he . . . when *that* happened, something happened to me, too. I kinda just went cold inside. And I didn't want anything to do with this family, especially my mom. She . . . they all . . . reminded me too much of my dad. So I just distanced myself. But at the same time I was so *furious*. I don't know why, but I was. So I figured I'd take it out on my mom . . . on people . . . or whoever . . . by getting wasted and flunking out of school and all that other stupid crap."

Kyle began sobbing again.

"Kyle, Kyle." Benjy scooted over and hugged her tightly. "Shhh, it's okay."

"No . . . it's . . . *not!*" Kyle sobbed.

"No, I guess it's not. But it will be, someday. Listen—I can't pretend to know what it's like to lose your dad. I can't imagine losing mine. But for whatever it's worth, you have this huge family, *our* family, who loves you and will always be there for you. You're not alone."

"Whatever," Kyle sniffed.

"You know, you really should sit down and talk to your mom about this stuff," Benjy said softly.

Kyle jerked back. "No!"

"Or Kass, or Kamille, or me, or whoever. You need to talk to *somebody*."

"What are you, my shrink now?"

Benjy pushed back a lock of her hair. "Yeah, well, someone's gotta make sure you don't go off the deep end again. It's pretty lame, how you keep doing that over and over again."

Kyle swiped at her eyes and laughed weakly. "I guess?"

There was a sudden commotion out in the hallway. Footsteps, yelling . . . then her mother rushed into the room.

Kyle sat up. "Mom? Is everything okay?" she said worriedly. "Is Bree—"

"Kass is about to have her baby!" Kat cried out. She looked happy and hysterical at the same time. "We've got to get down to the hospital, now! Where are my car keys? Has anyone seen my car keys? And my shoes, where are my shoes?"

Ohmigod, Kass's baby! "Can I go, too?" Kyle said meekly. "Even though I'm, uh, grounded for the next hundred years?"

Kat put her hands on her hips and glared at her. "No! Okay, yes. Just this once. But stay close. And don't get into any trouble, or I'm sending you away to live with your great-aunt Beatrice instead."

Ouch. "O-kay, I won't make a peep," Kyle said. "Thanks, Mom."

Kat's expression softened. She came over and gave Kyle a quick, fierce hug. "I could kill you for what you did, you know that," she said quietly. "But I love you. I will *always* love you, no matter what. You're my baby girl."

It was all Kyle could do not to start crying again.

Where in the hell was that Xanax, anyway?

FORTY-ONE

KASS

"THIS . . . HURTS . . . LIKE . . . *HELL*!" KASS SCREAMED.

Kat squeezed her hand. "Just breathe, darling! In and out, in and out! Just like they taught you in Lamaze!" she said cheerfully.

"*Screw* Lamaze! I need some drugs, *now*! Where is the goddamned *nurse*?"

Kass saw a worried glance pass between her mother and Beau. The two of them had been at the hospital for the last few hours, along with Kyle and Benjy, who had taken Bree down to the cafeteria for a snack.

Kass's due date wasn't for another couple of weeks, so she'd been taken by surprise when she'd woken up this morning with weird cramping sensations in her belly. She'd waited them out, thinking they would go away, figuring it was just the pad thai, sour cream and onion potato chips, and three chocolate mini donuts she'd eaten for dinner last night. But by evening they'd gotten more intense, so she'd called Dr. Chen. Who'd told her to come in right away because she was likely in labor.

And now the cramps were pure agony. Like ferocious lions gnawing and ripping at her stomach muscles from the inside. Which sounded delusional. But she *was* delusional, from the incredible, mind-numbing, apocalyptic waves of pain that had become her entire universe.

Why didn't someone *tell* her that childbirth was such torture? She would have taken an oath of celibacy a long, long time ago.

"Did I miss anything?" Kyle sauntered into the room, chugging a Red Bull.

"Where's Benjy and Bree?" Kat asked her.

"Buying crap in the gift shop. Your stomach's still ginormous, so I guess that the baby's not here yet," Kyle said to Kass.

"Fuck you, you little bitch," Kass said testily.

"Our Kassidy's a bit stressed right now," Kat explained.

"Can I get you anything, honey? Some more ice chips?" Beau offered to Kass.

"No! *Arggghhhhhh!* It *hurrrrrts!*"

"Maybe I'd better just go and leave you ladies to this," Beau whispered nervously to Kat.

"Okay, honey. Why don't you try Kamille again? I left her a bunch of texts and voice-mail messages," Kat whispered back.

"I *heard* that!" Kass yelled. "Kamille and I are no longer sisters, so please don't call her anymore! If you people *really* want to help, call the goddamned doctor and tell her to give me some goddamned drugs. *Now!*"

"You know, sweetie pie, when I had you girls, I did it completely naturally," Kat said in an infuriatingly calm voice. "Serenity, that was our midwife, and Rainbow, that was our doula—we used them for all three of you—really, really felt that the epidurals and so forth were counterproductive and not very good for the—"

Kass put her hands over her ears. Would her mother shut up about natural childbirth, already? Or just leave, so the doctors could come in with their high-tech arsenal of pharmaceuticals and knock Kass out cold? She could wake up, say, tomorrow morning, and they could just hand Annabella to her, all bundled up in a cozy receiving blanket and sleeping peacefully . . .

For a moment Kass desperately wished Kamille were here. They hadn't spoken in months or even seen each other. Kamille had moved out of their house right after the wedding disaster. She'd gotten her own apartment in West Hollywood and was busy with her modeling career. Once in a while, late at night, Kass found herself Googling Kamille's name. Various photos and stories would pop up with headlines like GETTING OVER CHASE, showing her at fancy, celebrity-studded events with different, homogenously cute guys—but no boyfriend.

Kamille hadn't tried to contact Kass, not even once. She had even insisted on their splitting up the Sunday Night Dinners so they wouldn't run into each other at the house. Kass had complied; what could she do, if Kamille hated her so much that she couldn't even sit down at the dinner table with her?

Even their birthdays, at the beginning and end of July, had been celebrated separately. It was like a divorce.

Kamille was—used to be—her best friend in the entire world. She was supposed to be here: holding Kass's hand, talking her down, and navigating her through the crazy, hellish, impossible, wonderful (okay, well, maybe not so wonderful) journey of childbirth.

As for Chase . . . Kass had gotten several calls and e-mails from him, offering financial assistance for the baby. Kass hadn't returned any of them. Maybe it was a nice gesture from a repentant asshole—or maybe it was another piece of sleight of hand. Or a way to keep her from pressing charges against him. Whatever. Kass wanted nothing to do with him ever again. She only hoped he would have the good sense to stay away from her and Annabella.

Another wave of pain. Kass screamed.

"Breathe, sweetheart," her mother said encouragingly. "Picture something happy, like Coco and Chanel when they were puppies. And breathe!" She winced. "Mmm, yikes."

"What is it?" Beau asked her, sounding concerned.

"Nothing. I, um . . . would you mind taking over for a sec, honey? I'm feeling a little queasy. I'm just going to step out for a bit and get some fresh air."

"Do you want me to get the doctor, darlin'?"

"No, no, I'm fine! Really! Just be the labor coach for a bit, okay?"

"Uh, okay."

Kass closed her eyes and tried to shut out the chattering voices—why was her mother acting like *she* was the patient

suddenly, when Kass was the one who was dying here?—
and picture the puppies. No. No good. All she could see was
Chanel scarfing down an entire coffee cake when she was two
months old and then throwing it up on Kass's lap.

Which made her want to throw up right this second . . .

"Now, *how* does this labor-coach thing work?" Beau was
asking Kyle. "I mean, should I tell her to breathe, or should I
breathe *with* her, or should I get the nurse, or the doctor, or—"

"I only went to like one Lamaze class with her," Kyle replied. "Yeah, the Candy Cane made us do all these breathing exercises, plus Kegels, too. You know, like, holding in your
pee?"

"Holding in your . . . pee?" Beau said uncomfortably.

"Don't you remember how to do this, Beau? From when
Benjy and Bree were born?" Kyle asked him.

"Not really, sweetheart. I think I fainted with Benjy, and I
might've fainted with Brianna, too."

"Lame," Kyle snorted.

"That *is* lame. Okay, you two, get the hell out of my way!"

Kass's eyes snapped open.

She couldn't believe it.

Kamille had come. She was standing in the doorway, looking impossibly gorgeous in a burgundy silk dress and black
stiletto heels.

"Ohmigod, Kamille!" Kass tried to sit up, but she couldn't.
"You're here! I'm so happy to see you! Ohmigod!" She began
crying.

"Whatever. I was at a movie premiere at Mann's, and I think
Robert Pattinson was about to ask me out, so you'd better be
grateful. How far apart are your contractions?"

Kass swiped her tears away. "Like every three minutes?"

"And how many centimeters are you?"

"The doctor said nine, almost ten."

"Holy shit, he's coming out any second now!"

"*She*. Kamille, I—"

"Shut the fuck up and breathe. Ready? Take my hand. Good! Now, breathe in . . . one, two, three, four . . ."

ALEXANDER DAVID ROMERO WAS BORN AT 11:06 P.M. that night. He weighed seven pounds six ounces and was twenty-one inches tall. Kass would have to save the name Annabella Grace for the next one . . . if and when she was insane enough to go through the experience of childbirth again.

Alex was perfect. And beautiful. And brilliant—Kass could tell by the way his tiny, almost translucent eyelids would flicker at the sound of her voice, as though he could already separate her from the rest of the loud, bubbly female energy in the room. He would no doubt go to Princeton or Yale someday. Or maybe USC like his mom and his grandpa David, so he could be close by, and so Kass could do his laundry every week when he came over for Sunday Night Dinners. He also had long, slender fingers—so maybe he would be a surgeon? Or a concert pianist?

"Ohmigod, he's so adorable!" Kamille said, for the hundredth time. "Can I hold him now, Kassie? Are you done holding him? Seriously, stop hogging, you are so selfish!"

"Kam, you just had him like a second ago," Kass pointed out.

Bree waved her hand in the air. "Me, me, me! What about me? I've gotta start practicing for babysitting!"

"I think he wants to cuddle with his old grandpa," Beau cooed. He leaned in and made a goofy face at Alex.

Benjy shook his head. "Nope, I think he wants his big brother. Besides, I only got to hold him once."

Kyle stepped in front of Benjy. "This is so awesome, having a baby bro. I can't wait to teach him how to—"

"*No!*" everyone said at once.

"I'm the grandma, so I get dibs," Kat said, reaching for Alex. "Besides, none of you are holding him right. You have to support his head and neck with your arm—like this—because he doesn't have any muscles back there yet," she added, demonstrating.

Just then, Alex's lips moved, and he made a tiny sputtering sound. There was a loud, adoring chorus of "awwwwwwww."

Kass wondered if he was ready to nurse again. He seemed to want to nurse almost constantly. "I think he's hungry. Do you guys think he's hungry?" she said out loud.

"I don't know. Put him on your boob and see what he does," Kamille suggested.

"Make sure he latches on correctly, Kassidy. Like this, let me show you." Kat started to unbutton her blouse.

"Mom! *Gross!*" Kyle grumbled.

"I think I'm gonna step out and grab a Coke," Benjy said, making a beeline for the doorway. "Can I get anybody anything?"

"Yeah, son, I think I'll join you. Let's give the ladies a little privacy," Beau agreed.

"Wait, Beau! You, too, Benjy!" Kat called out.

"Mom, *pssssst,*" Kamille said, pointing. Kat's black lace bra and part of a nipple were still showing.

"What? Oh, big deal, there's nothing here anyone hasn't seen," Kat said, buttoning up. "Anyway, I was going to wait to make the announcement, but since we're all here . . . for the first time in a long time, I might add . . ."

Sniffling, she wrapped one arm around Kamille and the other arm around Kass, squeezing them in an awkward three-way hug. Four-way, including Alex, who had fallen asleep on Kass's chest with milk dribbling down his chin and onto her toothpaste-green hospital gown. Kass was beginning to realize that parenting was going to be very messy, in more ways than one.

"So. I have some very happy news I want to share with everyone!" Kat went on.

Beau raised his eyebrows. "News? Do I know about this, sweetheart?"

"No, you don't. I was waiting for the right time."

"You're selling the restaurant and moving to a retirement home in Florida to enjoy your golden years," Kyle said with a straight face.

"Ha-ha, very funny. Actually, my news is . . . well, it's very relevant to *today,* to the arrival of our precious, darling little Alex. Because . . . *ta-da!* Alex is going to have a new aunt or uncle!" Kat exclaimed, throwing up her arms exuberantly.

Kass frowned. A new aunt or uncle. What did that even mean? Did her father have secret, illegitimate children that no one knew about until now? Did Beau? Kass was too exhausted from hours and hours of labor to sort out their complicated family tree.

Wait. Labor. Childbirth. Was Kat saying . . .

"Mom, you're not pregnant . . . are you?" Kass gasped.

Kat beamed. "I am! I'm three months along. The baby's due next February."

There was a stunned silence in the room. Then Alex woke up and began wailing. And everyone began talking at once.

"Mom, you're joking, right?" Kamille said loudly, trying to be heard above Alex's cries.

"Yeah, aren't you, like, too old?" Kyle added.

"My friend Portia's mom just had a baby, and she's like fifty," Bree said helpfully. "Portia said she did fertilizer treatments."

Poor Beau looked as though he was in shock. "But, sweetheart . . . darlin' . . . we didn't . . . that, is, this wasn't part of the . . . that is, how did this even . . ." His voice faltered.

Kat squeezed his hand. "I know we weren't planning on this, honey. But it just happened. I think it was maybe that morning we got that call from Irvine, and we ended up spending most of the day in bed, remember? I think we forgot to put in the—"

"*TMI!*" Kyle and Benjy yelled at the same time.

"What call from Irvine?" Kass said curiously. She rocked Alex back and forth, trying to calm him down. But he only cried louder.

"It's not important right now. That's another conversation for another time. For now, we can just be happy about my— that is, Beau's and my—baby news. Beau? Oh my gosh, *Beau*?"

But Beau had fainted. The top half of his body was draped awkwardly across the foot of Kass's bed. Benjy rushed over and tried to prop him up. "A little help here?" he said, panting. "Jeez, Dad needs to go on a diet, like, immediately."

Kamille leaned over to Kass. "Why does Mom always have to make it about her?" she whispered. "This is *our* day, *our* baby."

Kass grinned. "*Our* baby?"

"Well, yeah. You didn't think you were going to do this parenting thing alone, did you? I mean, you're good at math and econ and all your other nerd subjects. But you totally suck at people stuff."

"Gee, thanks, doll!"

"You're welcome, doll! Here, give him to me."

Without waiting for a reply, Kamille took Alex from Kass and readjusted his receiving blanket snugly. He snuffled and stopped crying. "See? He loves his aunt Kamille best. Don't you love your aunt Kamille best? Your aunt Kamille rocks!" she said, nuzzling Alex's nose.

Kass smiled wearily—she felt like she'd run a marathon—and leaned back against the pillows, taking in the scene around her. Kat and Benjy were trying to revive Beau, waving a bottle of hand sanitizer under his nose. Kyle was showing Bree how to change diapers, demonstrating with a linen dinner napkin and a blue "Congratulations on Your New Baby Boy!" teddy bear that she'd gotten in the gift store downstairs. Kamille was rocking Alex back and forth and singing "Express Yourself" to him lullaby-style, off-key.

Everything was back to normal again.

ACKNOWLEDGMENTS

First of all, a huge thank you to our families for all of their support.

To our mom, Kris Jenner, and Noelle Keshishian our fab management team!

To Jill Fritzo, Pearl Servat, and Gabe Walker at PMK*BNC, our publicity gurus.

And especially to Carla DiBello, Sheiva Ghasemzadeh, and Sydney Hitchcock. Thank you for helping us run our lives! You dolls are the best!

To Jen Haughton and Janie Marcus at BUZZMEDIA for all their great ideas.

Thanks to our glam squads: Joyce Bonelli, Rob Scheppy, Clyde Haygood, and Mario Dedivanovic.

An extra special thank you to our collaborator, Nancy Ohlin, for helping us make this book incredible.

To Lisa Sharkey, without your vision and passion *Dollhouse* wouldn't exist. Thank you, Doll!

To Tessa Woodward for her editing expertise and for getting us through this process!

To Carrie Feron, Lynn Grady, Liate Stehlik, and everyone else at William Morrow for championing our book.

To Shelby Meizlik and Seale Ballenger for all of their hard work on the publicity.

To Jimmy Iacobelli for our incredible cover!

To Joyce Wong for shepherding *Dollhouse* through production.

And, finally, to our William Morris Endeavor agents, Lance Klein and Mel Berger, for always being there for us.